Praise for Cynthia Ozick's

Antiquities

"This slim but by no means slight narrative is as cunning and rich as anything [Ozick has] written."
—*The Wall Street Journal*

"Age, we want to imagine, is what happens if we are lucky. But the reality is more complex. That is both the subject and the subtext of this novella, which is most resonant, perhaps, in how it never looks away from the slow but steady disintegration that awaits. Lloyd is a flawed and contradictory character, yet his vulnerability becomes its own kind of force." —*Los Angeles Times*

"[Ozick] can sing and she can rant; she can praise and she can castigate. . . . Striking. . . . Masterful."
—*The Boston Globe*

"In her fascinating new novella, *Antiquities*, Cynthia Ozick elevates the notion of an unreliable narrator to delightfully confusing new heights. Entertaining as it is at the level of pure storytelling, this fictional whirligig will have you rereading and rethinking to plumb its depths." —*Minneapolis Star Tribune*

CYNTHIA OZICK

Antiquities and Other Stories

Cynthia Ozick, a recipient of both the PEN/ Nabokov Award and the PEN/Malamud Award for fiction and a National Book Critics Circle winner for criticism, is the author of *Trust*, *The Messiah of Stockholm*, *The Shawl*, and *The Puttermesser Papers*. She lives in New York.

INTERNATIONAL

Antiquities and Other Stories

Cousin William

ANTIQUITIES

AND OTHER STORIES

★

Cynthia Ozick

Vintage International

VINTAGE BOOKS

A DIVISION OF PENGUIN RANDOM HOUSE LLC

NEW YORK

FIRST VINTAGE INTERNATIONAL EDITION, FEBRUARY 2022

Compilation copyright © 2022 by Cynthia Ozick

Portions of this work originally appeared in the following publications:
"The Bloodline of the Alkanas" in *Harper's Magazine* (February 2013); "A Hebrew
Sibyl" in *Granta* (November 2014); "Sin" in *The American Scholar* (September 2019);
and "The Coast of New Zealand" in *The New Yorker* (June 2021).

The Library of Congress has cataloged the Knopf edition as follows:
Names: Ozick, Cynthia, author.
Title: Antiquities / Cynthia Ozick.
Description: First edition. | New York : Alfred A. Knopf, 2021.
Identifiers: LCCN 2020025778 (print) | LCCN 2020025779 (ebook)
Classification: LCC PS3565.Z5 A85 2021 (print) | LCC PS3565.Z5 (ebook) |
DDC 813/.54—dc23
LC record available at https://lccn.loc.gov/2020025778
LC ebook record available at https://lccn.loc.gov/2020025779

Vintage International Trade Paperback ISBN: 978-0-593-31276-6
eBook ISBN: 978-0-593-31308-4

Frontispiece © UCL, The Petrie Museum of Egyptian Archaeology
Book design by Soonyoung Kwon

www.vintagebooks.com

Printed in the United States of America
1st Printing

TO

Melanie Jackson
who makes things happen

Contents

Antiquities and Other Stories

Antiquities

It is not hidden from thee, neither is it far off.
It is not in heaven, that thou shouldest say, Who shall
go up for us to heaven, and bring it unto us, that we
may hear it, and do it?
Neither is it beyond the sea, that thou shouldest say,
Who shall go over the sea for us, and bring it unto us,
that we may hear it, and do it?
But the word is very nigh unto thee, in thy mouth, and
in thy heart, that thou mayest do it.

—Deuteronomy 30: 11–14

My name is Lloyd Wilkinson Petrie, and I write on the
30th of April, 1949, at the behest of the Trustees of the
Temple Academy for Boys, an institution that saw its last
pupil thirty-four years ago. I must unfortunately report
that of the remaining Trustees, only seven (of twenty-
five) survive. Though well advanced in age myself, I am
the youngest, and the least infirm but for a tremor of the
left hand, yet capable enough at my Remington despite

long years of dependence on my secretary, Miss Margaret Stimmer (now deceased). In our continuing capacity as Trustees, we meet irregularly, contingent on health, here in my study, with its mullioned windows looking out on our old maples newly in leaf.

I call it my study, and why not? My father too kept a sequestered space by this name; his tone in speaking of it signaled a preference for solitude, much like my own. The others, who also have tenure here in Temple House, are pleased to designate their present apartments by those old classroom plaques: Fourth Form Alpha, Fifth Form Beta, and so forth. In this way the nomenclature of the Academy lives on, its various buildings having been converted for use in perpetuity as living quarters for the Trustees. It is notable that certain enhancing decorative efforts have been introduced to the interior of the structure, such as ornamental crown moldings, as well as the installation of an imposing crystal chandelier in each apartment. I believe my late wife would have approved of elaborate appointments of this kind, but the constant swaying and tinkling of these dangling beads and teardrops, at the lightest footstep or wafting of air, is in truth more annoyance than comfort.

The former staff are of course long gone, but we are well attended by a pair of robust young men and (lately) merely two matrons, one of foreign origin, and the refectory has been updated (as they term it) with a modern kitchen, including a sizable pantry. In addition, it is espe-

cially needful to recall that the common toilets and showers exclusively for the pupils' use, a disagreeable relic of
the Academy's early years, were torn down some time
ago. Only the chapel has been left as it was, unheated.

It was determined by consensus at our penultimate
meeting that what we are about to undertake shall not
be a history of the Academy. It is true that the existing
History, composed in 1915 at the moment of the Academy's demise, contains certain expressions that would not
be considered acceptable today. The local public library,
which gladly received this heartfelt work at the time,
will no longer permit it to stand on open shelves. Each
Trustee, however, owns a leather-bound copy, and may
for our immediate purpose consult it if needed, most
likely to retrieve a forgotten name.

Our agreed intent, then, is to produce an album of
remembrance, a collection of small memoirs meant to
stand out from the welter of the past—seven chapters of,
if I may borrow an old catchphrase, emotion recollected
in tranquility. When completed, it is to be placed in the
Academy vault at J. P. Morgan & Co., together with the
History and other mementos already deposited therein,
including the invaluable portrait of Henry James that
once adorned the chapel. It has always been a matter of
pride for us that the Academy's physical plant was constructed on what had been the property (a goodly acre-
age) of the Temple family, cousins to Henry James; it was

from these reputable Temples that the Academy gleaned its name. Unhappily, as recorded in the History, this circumstance has led to misunderstanding. That we were on occasion taken for a Mormon edifice, though risible, was difficulty enough. Most unfortunate was the too common suspicion that "Temple" signified something unpleasantly synagogical, so that on many a Sunday morning the chapel's windows (those precious panels of stained glass depicting the Jerusalem of Jesus's time) were discovered to have been smashed overnight. The youngest forms were regularly enlisted to sweep up the shards and stones.

How ironic were these ugly events, given that the Academy's spirit was premised on English religious and scholarly principles. Our teachers, vetted for probity and suitable church affiliation, were styled masters. Our pupils wore blazers embroidered with inspirational insignia, and caps to match. Football (on the British model) was hygienically encouraged. French, Latin, attendance at chapel, and horsemanship were all mandatory, and indeed our earliest headmaster was brought over, at a considerable wage, from Liverpool. And all that in the familiar greenery of Westchester County!

Yet I have thus far engaged in this overly hasty prologue without having spoken of my own lineage. I am, as stated above, a Petrie. We have had among us men distinguished in jurisprudence, and I retain in their original folders a selection of my grandfather's briefs, uncommonly impressive in that old copperplate hand, together with early letterheads, on fine linen paper, of the family firm, founded by his father. My own father in his youth left the firm briefly to pursue other interests, but was persuaded to return, and I have in my possession a sampling of his estimable contractual instruments, as well as a small private notebook crackling with grains of sand trapped in its worn and brittle spine. (Of this, more anon.) I am told that I have myself a certain prowess in the writing of prose, at least in the idiom appropriate to the law. And while these bloodline emblems of civic dedication hold pride of place in my heart, they do not reach the stratum of distinction, let alone of renown, of yet another Petrie.

Here I speak of William Matthew Flinders Petrie, knighted by the Queen, and more broadly known as the illustrious archaeologist Sir Flinders Petrie, who passed away in his home in a turbulent Jerusalem a scant seven years ago, and is partially interred in the Protestant Cemetery on Mount Zion. (I am obliged to say partially: his head he donated to the Royal College of Surgeons in London.) My father, in addition to his nearly lifelong devotion to the law (though that life was too brief), was enamored of ancient times, and of esoteric maps, and also of genealogy, and thereby successfully traced the degrees of our relationship to this extraordinary man. It is difficult, of course, to judge when a cousin of a certain distance becomes rather more of a stranger than a relation, but in my father's view there were reasons for his feelings of closeness.

I have intimated that my father impulsively broke away from the firm, to the shock of his parents, and more particularly the consternation of his young wife. (Among his papers I have found a browning newspaper clipping of this event, distressingly reported as a scandal.) He did in fact disappear in the blazingly hot summer of 1880, having gone in search of Cousin William (not yet Sir Flinders). At that time the press was infatuated with the spectacular excavations in Egypt, particularly the Great Pyramid of Giza, under the supervision of Cousin William, who was then a youthful prodigy of twenty-eight. My young father, newly married and destined for a vice-presidency, informing no one beforehand, had abruptly departed by steamship through Cadiz to Alexandria, after which he endured a miserable journey overland to the site of the excavations. It must be admitted that he did not go with empty pockets (he took with him money aplenty, privately arranging for further sums from a Spanish bank); nor could he be charged with absconding of funds. To a family firm such as ours, he was, after all, the heir.

It is from my discreet and quietly dispirited mother, in a burst of confession in her seventieth year, and seriously ailing, that I know something of the effects of this perfunctory escapade. With no inkling of its cause, my mother was left bewildered and distraught, and as week after week passed with no letter of explanation, and no notion of my father's destination, she believed herself in some inscrutable way to be the instigator of his flight, finding reason upon reason for blame. How could this be? Three months after a glorious winter wedding, all glittering whiteness without and within, the fresh snow still silken and unblemished, the nave lined with overflowing stands of white roses, rows of white pearls sewn into her dress, the groom glowing with ardor (and the paternal promise of an instant increase in earnings), how could this be? The Wilkinsons, indignant and fearful, took her away to weep alone in her childhood bedroom; her inchoate cries of guilt, and her unthinkable pleas for divorce, however confused and pitiful, had become too alarmingly public. They enrolled her for a time, she told me, in a well-appointed nursing home, to assure her calm, and to conceal their embarrassment, until the way-ward husband should return. And at length he did return, "brown as any darkie," as my mother described him, admi-rably resuming his place in the firm and at her side. Follow-ing my birth, and until the last hours of my mother's life, my father's unaccountable absence in the summer of 1880 was never again to be spoken of.

*

May 26, 1949. I have been compelled to leave off after a pe-riod of unexpected illness brought on by a sunny but uncharacteristically cold Spring, when it was decided to hold the most recent meeting of the Trustees outdoors, under the maples, on those ancient yet sturdy wooden benches originally situated there by the Temple family some eighty years before. There was to be a final consensual understanding of the nature of each Trustee's memoir: first, that it not exceed in length more than ten pages; second, that it be confined to an explicit happening lingering in memory and mood, and perhaps in influence, until this day; third, that it concern childhood only, and nothing beyond; fourth, that an implacably immovable date be set for completion, lest the indolence of some turn into general abandonment; and fifth, that it reflect accurately the atmosphere and principles of the Academy at the time in which the incident to be recounted had occurred. Ah, what callings-out of the past beneath those venerable trees!

I have failed to explain that each of the Trustees, by the terms of the Trust, and by design of the founders, must once himself have been a pupil of the Academy, and is thereby personally indebted to that past. Hence we all remember the reprehensible common showers. We all remember the sacking of the headmaster from Liverpool due to his inadequate accent and the misleading Cambridge degree that brought us those inferior vowels. (I sometimes ponder what poor Mr. Brackett-Lynn must have thought of our American vowels.) I might append here that of our seven extant Trustees, five are widowers, for whom marriage and family have compensated for early dolor, and two, having never married, are childless. I am glad to say that I am among the five, and am myself the father of a son. Eschewing the law, he long ago settled in California to pursue a career in, as he puts it, "film entertainment." (I am no philosopher, my leanings are wholly pragmatic, but I now and then contemplate how perverse is the cycle of familial traits, the capriciousness of an earlier generation unfathomably reappearing in a later one.) Despite this, we are by no means estranged, though the sputter of the long-distance telephone lines sometimes inhibits intimate talk.

Our conference in that redolent place under the burgeoning branches was cut short, as it happened, by a sudden heavy rainstorm, which accounts for my ten days in bed, when I took advantage of my temporary (though distressing) invalidism by reviewing the little I have set down thus far. How dismaying to note the wandering digressions, the lack of proportion, too much told here, not enough there, and how different from the logical composition of a legal brief! First the circumstance, then the argument invoking precedent, and finally the conclusion, all concise and in order, unburdened by excessive rumination. And I have not yet so much as approached the subject of my memoir, which I hope before long to touch on: the presence in the Academy of a fourth-form pupil preposterously called Ben-Zion Elefantin, his Christian name (so to speak) a puzzling provocation, his surname a repeated pretext for ridicule by merciless boys.

Of those boys at that distant time (and well afterward), nearly all were in a way unwanted half-orphans. Fathers, like mine, dead too soon, or mothers, like mine, too melancholy to tend to a son at home. And now that I speak again of my father, I must revert to the notebook referred to above, given to me by my mother directly after my father's death, together with certain other objects that I retain to this very day. The occasion was a rare holiday from school, permitted only that I might attend my father's obsequies, which chanced also to coincide with my tenth birthday. "Here are your father's toys," my mother said (satirically, as I later understood), and added that such things were fit only for a boy of my temperament, who, as she claimed, preferred mooning over chess pieces to skipping with other boys in fresh air. With the vague awareness of a child, I knew that long before my birth my father had journeyed alone to some faraway land, my mother being too ill to accompany him, and that he had returned with an exquisite gift to delight her: a gold ring in the shape of a scarab. (I never saw her wear it.) He brought with him, besides, an assemblage of ancient oddities—souvenirs, it may be, that had appealed to him during his travels. These had been neglected, dusty and untouched for years, in a glass-fronted cabinet in a corner of my father's study, until the morning following his funeral, when I was sent back to the Academy, carrying with me a bulky rattling pouch. I keep these curious treasures here, all in a row, on a shelf above my desk, just as they were, with the exception of one. (Of that one I will soon have more to say.)

As for the notebook, I hardly knew what to do with it. I made, I recall, some small attempts at reading it, but except for a cursory mention of buffaloes and elephants, there was nothing to interest a boy just turned ten, and I thrust it, along with the other things, into the pouch. Today, undeniably, and in light of my family's past, these much-faded writings are of overriding interest. The notebook has the dimensions of a playing card, no thicker than the width of my little finger. A crowded pencilled scribble in my father's recognizable hand, though plainly hurried. The opening pages disappointingly dull, consisting merely of a list drawn up in one lengthy column spilling over several sheets. Why my father kept this inventory I cannot tell. (It is troubling to think that perhaps he was intending to make a life of such implements, never to return to my mother.) Here I will try the reader's patience by transcribing only a small part of these jottings, viz.:

sledgehammers
handpicks
pickaxes
shovels

hoes
ropes
crowbars
sieves
buckets
baskets
mallets
sandbags
crates
turias
measuring tapes
wheelbarrows
line levels
theodolites
plaster
tents
horses

and so forth, though of horses he would have more to observe. What most struck my father on his arrival amid the dust and debris and the volcanic heat and the ceaseless jabber of the fellahin, all of them naked to the waist, was the stench of the horses' droppings, melting and sizzling in the baking sand; incongruous as it might be, he was all at once reminded of those long-ago riding lessons at the Academy (already well established in my father's time) purported to be requisite among a young man's skills. How strange, he thought, that over such a great distance, and in such disparate scenes, the smell should be exactly the same!

In view of his warm admiration for Cousin William, I fear that my father was disheartened by his first encounter with this remarkable young man, so close in age to his own (my father was then approaching his thirty-first birthday). He was not welcomed as he had hoped to be. To begin with, he was taken aback by his cousin's appearance: the skin of the brow already markedly lined, while the hint of a beard was late in its growth. He seemed simultaneously both a youth and a seasoned elder. His authority was innate and absolute. But for my father, most uncanny of all was this: to look into the face of Cousin William was akin to gazing into a mirror. The brilliant blue of the eye was the same, though set off against bronze, and the bold cast of the jaw, with its slight yet telltale prognathic ridge (which I too have inherited), was unmistakably famil-ial. Yet though Cousin William was tall, my father was significantly taller, and when he was unceremoniously conscripted and sent to toil among the dark and puny fellahin, he loomed over them, he records, like a white pillar. He had in his enthusiasm immediately presented his genealogical findings to his cousin, but was abruptly warned that such fooleries were irrelevant to the work at hand. You can stay, Cousin William told him, if you are willing to pick up a spade. And if you are willing to pay for your keep.

Under the weight and strain of the long, groaning measuring chains, and his labors with pickaxe and ropes, my father soon threw off his own shirt and wound it around his head as a shelter from the blasting Levantine sun. He gradually became indistinguishable in complexion from his companions, who churned around him in their dusky swarms; he even learned a few words of their language. He grew used to the daylong sound of the great sieves skittering and shuddering like tireless dice. Hauling their laden baskets, the women and children crawled to and fro as mindlessly as a procession of beetles. The children looked underfed, and the women in their ragged tunics, or whatever they were, seemed to my father hardly women at all. His tent at night was invaded by insects of inconceivable size. In daylight, wherever the ubiquitous sand with its scatterings of wild brush and grasses gave way to more familiar vegetation, the earth itself had a reddish tint. And in those ferociously brilliant sunsets, even the sand turned red.

My father did indeed pay for his keep, and more: two extra horses, the photographic equipment soon to arrive from Germany, and an occasional repast for the youngest children, much frowned on for its disruption of duty. And still my father was joyful in those infrequent intervals when Cousin William was inclined to engage with him, most usually to lament an impending shortfall of means: after all, they were two civilized men in happy possession of the selfsame civilized tongue! There were even times when Cousin William spoke thrillingly of his plans for the decades ahead: he would search in the Holy Land for all those famed yet lost and buried Biblical cities, among them Lachish and Hinnom, and so many storied others. He meant one day, he said, to open the womb of the land that was the mother of true religion.

In late August, when the season of excavation was brought to a close, my father turned to an unused page in his notebook and requested that Cousin William inscribe it. And here it is now, clear under my present gaze: "From Petrie to Petrie, Giza, Egypt, 1880." And my father's comment below: "Proof that we are of the same blood."

With nothing useful to occupy him now, my father hired a boatman to ferry him across the Nile to Cairo, where he purchased some proper clothing and had a proper bath and settled, like any idle pleasure-seeker, in a lavish hotel, where, I presume, he pondered his fate and his future. Here there is nothing introspective, but for a single word, joined by a question mark: "Ethel?" (My mother's name.) What follows is a brief account of sailing down the Nile in a felucca, together with a chattering guide, all very much in the vein of a commonplace travelogue. Indeed, it reads as if copied from a Baedeker. He describes the green of the water, a massive colony of storks dipping their beaks, a glimpse of an occasional water buffalo, and on the opposite bank, as they were nearing the

First Cataract at Aswan, a series of boulders on the fringe of what (so the guide informed him) was an island with a history of its own, littered with the vestigial ruins of forgotten worship. The boulders were huge and gray, like the backs of a herd of elephants, and beyond them a palm-studded outgrowth. But it was not for these vast vertebrae that the island was called Elephantine, my father learned; it had, it was said, the shape of a tusk. And here he wrote bluntly in his notebook: "So much for the Nile."

In Cairo he loitered discontentedly, as he admits, too often pestered by street vendors pressing on him what purported to be invaluable relics of this era and that, or original bits of limestone casing salvaged from a nearby pyramid. He passed them by, but not always. He was tempted to believe in material authenticity; Cousin William had inspired him. (At this juncture it behooves me to remark that my father never again came into the presence of Sir Flinders Petrie, though for the remainder of his life he read of Cousin William's archaeological repute with persistent and considerable pride.)

To fill those desolate hours—in the sparseness of his final passages he hardly ever speaks of going home—my father began to frequent the souks with their luring rows of antiquities shops, where he saw and he bought, and sometimes believed, and sometimes did not. The dealers were pleased to educate him. Some objects were precious but likely looted. Others were forgeries, and still others purposeful pretenders from small local factories staffed by assiduous carvers and sculptors; caution was necessary. Let the buyer beware! Still, my father saw and bought, saw and bought, and in one honest shop chose a ring of true gold, in the shape of a scarab, which the merchant assured him, with a wink of his eye, had once belonged not to Queen Nefertiti, but to one of her handmaidens, and even if not, it was anyhow genuine gold. (I must note it again: though this very ring was kept with other such ornaments in a china bowl on her dresser, I never once saw it on my mother's finger.)

And then it was mid-September, and my father came home to my mother, and to his destiny in the family firm.

*

June 17, 1949. The truth is that I am discouraged. I have had to stop and reread and relentlessly subject to sober judgment the narrative above, which because of my father's factual flatness (that meticulous list of tools and devices!) was, to my surprise, less harrowing than I had supposed. My father, as I have already observed, was not given to introspection or disclosure. The motive for his precipitous decamping has never been uncovered, and I believe never will be. My son in Los Angeles, recently learning of this long-hidden chronicle, has asked to inspect it, with the end in mind of transforming its scenes (the Great

Pyramid, the Nile, the souks of Cairo, et al.) into some noisome motion picture adventure. He expresses particular interest in my mother's travail, and has gone so far as to suggest a notable actress to embody it. As one would expect, I have categorically refused.

All this contention, thrashed out on the telephone, has left me demoralized. But I am far more apprehensive of what lies ahead: the memoir itself, which I recognize I have not yet adequately adumbrated. Since I have no informing scrawl to rely on, as heretofore, it is as if I must excavate, as in a desert, what lies far below and has no wish to emerge—to wit, my boyhood emotions. And by now I cannot escape telling of my racking affections for Ben-Zion Elefantin. That my friendship with him, unlikely as it was, would taint me, I knew. Willy-nilly, I must in earnest soon begin.

The reader will permit me a word, however, about my colleagues in this venture. If I have been delinquent in my progress herein (out of embarrassment, perhaps, or dread), I am not alone. You will recall that among the preparations for these memoirs, a specific finishing date was strictly agreed on. This somewhat threatening clause was proposed by the pair of fellow Trustees I have characterized as unmarried and childless, hence somewhat childlike themselves. They warned, you will remember, of indolence, intending a charge of procrastination leading to evasion, and of course it came as an accusation crudely directed against my own such tendencies. Yet there is no sign that either one of these gentlemen has written so much as a line. They wake late, apparently giving much attention to their dress. The noticeably younger one is a bit of a dandy, with his colorful vests and his showy silk ties. The two of them dawdle over breakfast in one or the other's apartment (they are wanting in any sense of privacy), and in these long and pleasant summer afternoons sit out under the maples, reading incomprehensible poetry in breathless half-whispers (Gerard Manley Hopkins, I believe, of whom I am satisfied to know nothing). Observing this duo of scrawny elders with their walkers beside them, one our sole nonagenarian, how can I not suppose their theatrics to be but a hollow affectation of youth? And it is certainly indolence. How can I proceed with my own memoir if others take theirs so lightly? Our project, after all, is intended solely to honor the Academy, and merits sincere diligence, humbling though this may be.

As it happens, my own diligence, or my occasional lack of it these warm June days when I am overcome by an unconquerable need to nap, can always be detected. I refer to the tapping of my Remington. Even with my door shut, its clatter can be heard throughout the corridors of Temple House. The others, confined to their silent fountain pens, are not subject to such audible surveillance. I am, as I say, a practical man, and early on took advantage of an opportunity that allowed me to acquire this useful skill. Yet luckily, until her unhappy demise seven years ago, I have never had to do without the competence (and may I add the sweetness?) of Miss Margaret Stimmer. She came to us at the age of eighteen, in response to a notice in the Tribune, and already formidably equipped with a sure command of shorthand. She confessed that she had not yet mastered the typewriter but was ready to learn, and rather winningly flourished before me a manual of instructions purchased that very day. I agreed to take her on provisionally, on the condition that she within three weeks reach a designated speed of performance. Her eagerness was persuasive, and she was winning in other ways: spirited brown eyes, and dangling brown curls, and cheeks charmingly pink—wholly in the absence, I was certain, of any aid of artifice. I observed her slender white fingers, hour after hour, dancing more and more agilely over the keys. Miss Margaret Stimmer served as my secretary for many years, until the death of my dear wife, when she became, and remained, my very good friend.

And it is to her that I owe my own facility at the typewriter. Long after she had grown proficient, she kept in one of the lower drawers of her desk, perhaps as a kind of talisman of her felicitous arrival, the manual of instruction that brought her to us. There were times, when she and all others were gone for the day, and our offices were unpeopled and hushed, in my capacity as partner (my father had seen to my promotion soon after the birth of my son) I would stay behind to review the work of some newly hired young attorney. And often enough what I saw in those regrettable papers would lead me to reflect on the future of the firm: if, say, we were to fall on hard times and were forced to retrench? and if such an eventuality might one day compel me to do without a secretary? A practical man must be resourceful, so that now and then in those quiet nights, at a late and lonely hour, I would— delicately and hesitantly—remove from the lower drawer of Miss Margaret Stimmer's desk that well-worn manual, according to whose guidance I studied and practiced, studied and practiced, repeating difficult combinations again and again. And then I would restore the manual to its drawer, lingering over whatever else might be therein: Miss Margaret Stimmer's fresh daily handkerchiefs, with their particular fragrance, and (somewhat to my disappointment) a compact of rouge, with its little round mirror, and a forgotten pair of lemon-colored chamois gloves. It was pleasant then to picture those nimble white fingers sliding easily into their five clinging tunnels—and once I myself attempted to fit my far thicker and clumsier fingers into Miss Margaret Stimmer's gloves. But it could not be done.

Then let it be noted once more: it is solely because of Miss Margaret Stimmer's fortuitous presence and my consequent expertise at the typewriter, that my colleagues are able to ascertain my progress in the composition of this memoir, while I am entirely in the dark about theirs.

*

June 22, 1949. I have at long last decided to offer a description, as far as I am able, of my father's collection. To my knowledge, it has never been properly appraised, as it ought to have been, by any reputable scholar; but for the purpose of this memoir I scarcely think this remiss. Each piece, or so I speculate, was selected chiefly to gratify my father's interest and adoration, and if the utility of each remained a mystery, so much the better. Many of these pieces, and pieces they are, are instantly identifiable: clay lamps, jugs with handles like ears and spouts like the mouth of a fish, amulets, female figurines, and the like, but many are baffling. All are in a way miniature, either because they are parts broken off from a whole, or were conceived on this small scale. I had carried them to the Academy, as I earlier mentioned, with no notion of where I could keep them. Not on display in my cold little fifth-form cell, like the foolish feminine bric-a-brac we had at home: this would surely invite jeers. Happily, my writing table had beneath it a small cabinet with wooden doors, with its own lock and key, in which I stored my modest necessities, and I installed them there, still in their pouch— all but one artifact, taller than the others, and untypically intact, only because the bits had been almost seamlessly sealed in place by some master restorer's unknown hand. Its storkish height prevented my concealing it with the others; the height of the shelves was too low. Instead, I deposited it under my bed in a shoebox that had no lid and covered it with a pair of woolen socks.

What am I to call this object? It was a jug like other jugs (I mean a container), but more striking: it was made in the shape of a stork. Its breast was the breast of a stork, high and arched. Its spout was a stork's long tapering bill that flowed from a head with an emerald eye. By emerald I intend not merely the color, but the veritable gem itself, yet only on one side of the head. The other showed an empty socket. The legs were folded at the knee, as if kneeling in water, and it was these knees, showing minute specks of their original red, that formed the object's base. Under the base, when I turned it over, were odd scratchings, grooves worn shallow by some forgotten alphabet.

In the days following my father's burial, or, rather, in the half-dark of the nights when the Academy slept and my door was shut, it became my clandestine habit to pluck this object from its cradle and contemplate its meaning for my father. Why had it attracted him, and why had he brought it from that faraway land? Did he imagine it to be a welcome if exotic ornament for domestic display, certain to please my mother? But I saw that my mother scorned it—she who was otherwise partial to polished decorative vases on this and that decorative little table; and at last my father hid it away. It belonged, she said, to his "mad episode," an episode rarely alluded to and never defined. Or perhaps it was only that she judged it too crude and broken, with its missing eye.

In the dim corridor light that seeped under my door the emerald eye glittered, while the blind eye seemed to vanish away. For a reason I could not say then, and still cannot say now, an uncommon image came to me: I thought of a chalice. But a stork cannot be a chalice. So I called this curious thing by the name its birdlike spirit evoked: I called it a beaker. And because of the solitary nature of my cell I had little fear of its discovery.

*

June 23, 1949. It was considered one of the Academy's attractions that each pupil should have his own room, to be fully in his charge, and also to compel him to undergo the discipline of cleaning it daily and changing his personal bedsheets every Saturday morning. (At a later date, when as Trustee it became my duty to assess expenses, I saw how these youthful responsibilities conveniently lessened the need for house maids.) The reader will have seen that I speak of my cell. This term was introduced to us with the arrival of Mr. Canterbury, the new headmaster recruited to replace poor Mr. Brackett-Lynn. Mr. Canterbury had pursued divinity studies at Oxford; his accent was pronounced satisfactory. He was expected to teach Latin and English Poetry, to maintain order and propriety, and also to preside over chapel. His first innovation was to install a carpet over the bare cold floor of his study, and also to secure it with lock and key. His aim above all, he said, was to eliminate certain American vulgarities and to elevate our language in general. When some of the masters, and nearly all of the pupils, objected to "cell" for its aura of incarceration, he insisted that its source was, rather, ecclesial and poetical, and for proof cited Coleridge's "the hall as silent as a cell," whereas, he retorted, our halls rivaled in noise a dungeon of blacksmiths with hammer and tongs. I am glad to say that "cell" did not last, and neither did Mr. Canterbury. His long-serving successor was the Reverend Henry McLeod Greenhill, of Boston, who later assisted in the shutting of the Academy, and whose personal library we still retain following his passing soon afterward.

In this connection, and in one of those anomalies of unexpected confluence, the phrase "hammer and tongs" set down above was repeated a very few hours later, via a most distasteful occurrence. I was accosted at the dinner hour by three of my colleagues, who had formed a committee to denounce me. I was accused of making a racket, of disturbing the peace, of interfering with well-earned sleep, and finally of wielding hammer and tongs (these very words) at unconscionable hours. It is true that on certain days when I have, to my dismay, lost an entire afternoon through napping too long, my conscience has impelled me to take up my memoir somewhat past midnight. (Despite such efforts I remain acutely aware that beyond having uttered the name, I have yet to properly acquaint the reader with my unusual attachment to Ben-Zion Elefantin.)

In fine: I have been upbraided (I mean verbally assaulted) for the nocturnal use of my Remington, which in fact I associate most deeply with remembrance of those long-ago nights in my office. (I may have omitted to mention that the machine I own now is the very one used for many years by Miss Margaret Stimmer.) Yet I can hardly believe it is the sound of my energetic tapping that offends. Nor is it altogether envy of a skill the others do not possess. It is, instead, naked resentment: I alone appear to have progressed with my memoir, and they, or so I surmise, have been shamefully idle.

And here it may be pertinent to note that two of my three accusers are the very gentlemen already characterized in these pages as childish; and so, more and more manifestly, they are. As for the third offender, he is, shall we say, the kind of nonentity that follows the herd.

Same day, later. An architectural aside. I have alluded to the shutting of the Academy. The renovations that followed, in bringing about our present-day Temple House, required that four or five, and in one instance six, of these unheated cells be combined (i.e., razed) to create a single larger space to accommodate each new apartment. As a result, we now find ourselves in considerable comfort in the identical site of our early misery.

I ought also to add a word about the above-referenced library. The remodeling work necessitated the destruction of an area that from the earliest days of the Academy has always served as the headmaster's personal quarters, including the office to which pupils were summoned. It was in this sanctuary that Reverend Greenhill's library was kept. That it appeared as a bequest to the Trustees in his will was, it must be admitted, troublesome. Though his predecessors were piously, or let us say outwardly, celibate, Reverend Greenhill had come to us as a widower. He prided in his library as if (so goes the saying) it had sprung from his loins. It was his great pleasure and his even greater treasure. But to speak plainly, for the Trustees, at that time twenty-five strong and mainly men of business and law, what were we to do with these scores of volumes of theology and Greek and other such scholarly exotica? Of the several curators of the various institutes to which we offered this trove, all rejected it as an amateur's collection, hardly unique and easily duplicated, much of it uselessly outdated. Today it is stored on dozens of shelves in the kitchen pantry. Lately, I have been leafing through a few of these old things, with their curled and speckled pages, and in one, to my delight and amazement,

I discovered a paragraph naming Sir Flinders Petrie! I have since removed this book (The Development of Palestine Exploration, by one Frederick Jones Bliss, dated 1906) and display it here in my study, as a suitable companion to my father's keepsakes. I believe it would have pleased him to see it there.

*

June 26, 1949. Once again I have been reviewing these reflections, only to increase my despondency. All is maundering, all is higgledy-piggledy, nowhere do I find consecutive logic. For this reason I have turned to my personal copy of the History, hoping to come under its superior influence. Unlike our present project, this far more compendious work was composed by committee, with the benefit of a number of orderly minds contributing both to substance and style. It is in the spirit of research, in fact, that I am immersed in these crisply written chapters: I have sought to learn whether the Academy in its lengthening past has ever permitted the enrollment of Jewish pupils. A certain Claude Montefiore, of the English Montefiores, did attend in 1866, but only briefly, during his father's consular mission; but no others since, including up to my own father's time.

The absence of Jewish pupils, however, does not prevent the History from mentioning Jews, which it does fairly often, in general terms, with satirical or otherwise jesting comments on the Hebrew character. There is always, I believe, a kernel of truth in these commonplace disparagements. For instance, in my own Academy years I saw for myself how inbred is that notorious Israelite clannishness. Mr. Canterbury, as one would expect, held on to our traditional policy of exclusion, but with the coming of the Reverend Greenhill, some half-dozen or so Jewish boys were admitted, and I grew to know them well, if from a distance, lest I too be shunned. What was most remarkable about these unaccustomed newcomers, I observed, was not simply that they were Jews, or were said to be Jews, or acknowledged themselves (always diffidently) to be Jews. Yet in their appearance, and their ways, they were like everyone else: hardy on the football field (as I, incidentally, was not), hair dribbling over their eyes (a local fad), and in chapel yawning and restless and making faces, like the rest of us, at the departing Mr. Canterbury. Even their names were not noticeably distinctive, though one of them, Ned Greenhill, could scarcely have been related to Reverend Greenhill! This Ned, as it happens, and despite his effort to conceal it, was exceptional in Latin, becoming thereby a favorite of Reverend Greenhill, who held him up as a model. (An invidious rumor had it that Reverend Greenhill was privately tutoring him in Greek.) This alone was enough to encourage our avoidance, and anyhow these Hebrews did have the habit of clinging to their own. It has nevertheless since occurred to me that this unseemly huddling may have been the result, not the cause, of our open contempt. To speak to a Jew would be to lose one's place in our boyish hierarchy.

(Many years later, I would now and again lunch at the Oyster Bar with Ned Greenhill, by then a judge in the Southern District of New York. Our families, it goes without saying, never met.)

*

June 28, 1949. Upon my retirement from the law, I took away with me a very few objects evocative of my days and nights in that long-familar office, where my father and his father too had toiled: Miss Margaret Stimmer's machine, of course (with her permission), and also several small or middling items belonging originally to my grandfather, including a charming rocking-horse blotter made of green quartz, a weighty brass notary sealing device with its swan's-neck lever, and even a little bottle of India ink with a rubber stopper, once used to append indelible signatures to official documents. All these I still have with me here in my study, and a few, like the rocking-horse blotter and the India ink, I keep within daily sight on my writing table. (This ink, by the way, has never fully evaporated, thanks to its rubber stopper, and is as fluid as it was the day the bottle was first opened.) The reader may suppose that here I echo my father and his penchant for collecting; but this is hardly the case. All these oddments are quiet emblems of nostalgic reminiscence, whereas my father's things could mean nothing personal to him, being cryptic signals from an unknowable past. What can scratchings on the base of a beaker tell? If such an object does own a familial history, however remote, it is certainly not my father's. It is possible, I presume, that this very beaker may carry his emotion in having once enjoyed a close association with Sir Flinders Petrie, and may stand as an expression of the altogether different life my father might have lived had he succumbed to temptation and continued in his cousin's path. If so, out of respect for my mother's memory, I cannot follow him there.

Thinking back, I am much moved to recall that the day I made Miss Margaret Stimmer's typewriter my own was the very day I permitted myself to call her Peg.

*

Fourth of July, 1949. The cell opposite mine (this was still within Mr. Canterbury's tenure), with the corridor between us, was for a long time unoccupied. The boy it belonged to had contracted tuberculosis, which for many weeks went unrecognized. There was much illness all around in those unbearably cold winter days, and our cells, as previously remarked, were unheated. Nearly everyone, the masters included, was subject to running noses and chronic coughing. Still, no one coughed with the vehemence and persistence of the pupil in the cell across from mine. I had no choice save to suffer through it; it kept me awake night after night. Mr. Canterbury was finally persuaded to inform the boy's guardian, who came and took him away. He never returned, and all we knew further of him was that a lawsuit was somehow involved. It was then that Mr. Canterbury disappeared from the Academy, and Reverend Greenhill arrived, and with him a welcome innovation: a feather quilt for each boy's bed. At the same time, he arranged for the halls to be heated (an amenity primitive by present standards); and one morning in chapel he instructed us to keep our doors open to let in the warmth, and also, he admonished, to invite the equal warmth of pleasant social discourse. (How odd to be remembering the cold, when the temperature today approaches 100 degrees!)

But soon another pupil lay in what had been the sick boy's bed. His door was often closed. Either he had come too late to be apprised of the new rule, or he chose to ignore it. Since he was in the form below mine, and attended different classes, I glimpsed him only intermittently, in the refectory or in chapel. His behavior in both these circumstances was odd. I never saw him eat a normal dinner. He seemed to live on bread and milk and hard-boiled eggs, and he always sat by himself. In chapel, even when reprimanded, he never removed his cap. In fact, I never saw him without it. And while the rest of us whispered and snickered and pretended to sneeze during the reading of the Gospel and all through the sermon, he seemed rigidly attentive. He joined in the singing of a certain few hymns, but for others he was willfully silent. In appearance he was also uncommon. He was so thin as to approach the skeletal (his legs were nearer to bone than flesh), and this I attributed to his sparseness of diet. His complexion was what I believe is called olive, of the kind known to characterize the Mediterranean and Levantine peoples; but in contrast to this deficit of natural ruddiness, his hair was astoundingly red. And not the red of the Irish. As I write, I am put in mind of my father's description of the red earth of his days with Cousin William: deeper and denser and more otherworldly than any commonplace Celtic red.

He had come to us shortly after that influx of Jews, but he hardly seemed one of them, and they too, as we all did, were wary of everything about him, particularly his outlandish names, both the first and the last, which were all it was possible to know of him. There were some, playing on his surname, who joked that he was undoubtedly a Jew, given the elephantine length of his nose. To these jibes he said nothing, and merely turned away. And others (the more rowdy among us) claimed that only a Jew would flaunt Zion so brazenly, forgetting that the Psalms recited in chapel, which so frequently invoked Zion, were part and parcel of our Christian worship. I was particularly alert to this error, since on the Wilkinson side there can be found (too many, my father said) evangelical pietists who cling ardently to Zion, a few of whom are bizarrely devoted to speaking in tongues. And in the Petrie line too there have been numerous Old Testament appellations; we were once a sober crew of Abrahams and Nathans and Samuels, all of them proper Christians.

But there was more than Ben-Zion Elefantin's unusual name to irritate conventional expectations. Though rarely heard, his voice was perplexing. It had in it a pale echo of Mr. Canterbury's admirable vowels, but also an alien turn of the consonants, suggesting a combination of foreignisms—where exactly was he from? And why was he a full semester behind, in the form below mine, despite the fact, as I later learned, that at nearly twelve he was two years older than I? And was he mad, or merely a liar? I came, in time, to think the latter, though I was, I confess, something of a liar myself, feigning injuries of every variety in order to evade the football field. Mr. Canterbury had been inclined to expose me, and for punishment doubled my obligations to football and riding (like my father before me, I was greatly averse to horses); but Reverend Greenhill's view was that one's duty to God did not necessarily include kicking and galloping, and he sent me off to do as I pleased, as long as it harmed neither man nor beast.

What it pleased me to do during those football afternoons when the halls were deserted, and the shouting was distant and muffled, was to sit on my bed with my chessboard before me, while hoping to outwit a phantom opponent. On the memorable day I will now record, my door, according to protocol, was ajar, and when I looked up from my wooden troops, I saw Ben-Zion Elefantin standing there. Without speaking a word, he hopped on the bed to face me, and began maneuvering first a knight, and then a rook, and finally a queen, and I heard him say, very quietly, indeed humbly, If you don't mind, checkmate. I asked him then whether he, like me at that hour, had explicit permission to exempt himself from the field. He seemed to consider this for a moment, and said, with unhurried directness, I have no interest in that. I thought it was natural to inquire, since he was new to the Academy, in what other activity he did take interest. Chapel, he said. I found this unlikely; no boy I knew regarded chapel as anything other than a morning of aching tedium. Are you religious, I asked. The word does not apply, he said, at least not in the sense you intend. It was a strange way of speaking; no normal boy spoke like a book. I asked where he had been to school before coming to us. Oh, he said, many schools, in many places, but I never stay long, and until now was never taught fractions. Is that why, I asked, they've put you in fourth? Oh, he said, it hardly matters where I am put, before long they will call me away. Thank you, he said, for the pleasure of the game. And then he left me and went back to his room and shut the door.

*

July 5, 1949. Aside from yesterday's stifling weather (continuing at 97 degrees today), which compelled my breaking off my narrative too abruptly, the Fourth of July could not have been more disagreeable. A group of unruly youths from a neighboring town notorious for its shabbiness invaded our grounds, overturned the handsome old benches under the maples, and, targeting our windows, tossed deafening volleys of firecrackers while shouting obscenities. To such depths has patriotism fallen. Those warlike fumes have seeped into my study, where they hover still, stirred by useless electrical fans (I have two, and they do nothing to alleviate the abominable heat). One of the household staff, a half-incomprehensible native of Vienna, I suppose intending to please, made a pitiful attempt to celebrate the holiday by presenting us with what she calls a Sacher torte, an absurdly irrelevant cake of some kind, overly sugared; but one can expect nothing comfortably familiar from this postwar flotsam and jetsam. As for the disastrous war itself, our hard-won victory on two fronts is by now four years gone, yet there are some who even today decline to forgive President

Roosevelt for, as they say, putting Americans at risk for the sake of saving the Jews. There may be, as always, the usual kernel of truth in this; but that the Jews weren't saved in any event (nor many others, for that matter) is proof of the overall purposelessness of that war. Hitler and Stalin, Tweedledum and Tweedledee. The newspapers are rife with grotesque tales of camps and ovens; one hardly knows what to believe, and I am nowadays drawn far less to these public contentions than to my own reflections. This is not to say that I am not proud of my son's participation in the war, though it lacked a certain manliness, I mean of exposure to danger, since he was never on the battlefield, but rather in a printing office—something to do with a publication for soldiers and sailors.

In connection with which, the reader will have observed that save for her passing, I have had little to say of my late dear wife, an avid lover, as I earlier indicated, of the decorative arts; I hope to correct this here. Yet Miranda's influence on our son was perhaps too pressing, and may have led him to his current frivolous preoccupations in California. Miranda herself was fond of such fanciful trivia, in the form of heading the flower committee of her Women's Club and numerous like pursuits, e.g., her accumulation of painted bowls and porcelain figurines in the Japanese style: a man in a flat hat drawing a bucket out of a well, a sloe-eyed woman posed on a bridge. More to the point, she was much interested in the lives of Carole Lombard and Myrna Loy, those so-called "stars" of cinema. She liked to joke that I had married her only because of her clear resemblance to Myrna Loy, which was certainly not the case; at the time I scarcely knew the name. Miranda was indeed very pretty, but the reason for our marriage, of which our son was the premature consequence, remains entirely private. Nor can I deny that her parents insisted on it.

I see that I have again digressed, and though I mean to enlighten the reader further with regard to Ben-Zion Elefantin, I detect at this moment a relieving breath of a breeze beyond the sultry movements of the fans. The evening cool has begun, and I am off to walk in its respite. Yet first I must secure this manuscript before leaving my study. Until its completion I keep it for privacy in an unidentifiable box with a lid. It once held my father's cigars, and their old aroma lingers still.

*

July 6, 1949. A calamity, an outburst of childish spite. An inconceivable act of vengeance. It could not have been spontaneous; it had to have been carefully plotted, my habits noted, my comings and goings spied on. My colleagues have long been aware that at the close of these brutal equatorial days, I have taken to tracing the paths circling the maples, where wisps of evening airs rustle in their leaves. (Early this morning the staff, I am relieved to say, righted the benches and disposed of the debris, including a considerable scattering of beer bottles.)

At such times it is good to walk and think, walk and think. How am I to tell more of Ben-Zion Elefantin? I cannot reveal him in the way of dialogue (a practice my son puts his trust in, he informs me, as an aspiring screenwriter). I have not that gift or inclination. Nor am I certain it will finally be possible to reveal Ben-Zion Elefantin by any narrative device. It may be that all I knew of him was fabrication or delusion.

I wandered thusly, mulling these enigmas, for half an hour or so, and then returned to my study refreshed, intending despite the late hour to set down my thoughts. What I saw before me—saw in one hideous instant—was a scene of ghastly vandalism. On the surface of my writing table stood my little bottle of India ink, uncorked, with its rubber stopper prone beside it. Someone—someone!—had spilled its contents over the body of my Remington, obliterating the letters on its keys and wetting the roller so repulsively that it gleamed like some slithering black slime. Miss Margaret Stimmer's Remington violated, the very machine, now mine, once touched by her prancing fingers, and all I have left to remind me of my sweet Peg.

★

July 8, 1949. The reader will have noted that the forego-
ing paragraphs have been written, perforce, in longhand, and at various intervals, in various states of mind.
Hedda of the kitchen staff (it was she who inspired the
Sacher torte), seeing my distress, volunteered to take
the despoiled Remington away in an attempt to clean
it. She assured me that vinegar would do the job well
enough, and so it mostly has, if not to my full satisfac-
tion. The balls of my fingers still turn black from the keys,
and the friction of typing sends up a fine mist of charcoal-
like dust to coat my eyeglasses and nose. Hedda calms me
with the promise that all this will not persist, and advises
patience, or else a second vinegar bath. That the mecha-
nism has not been irreparably harmed hardly assuages my
shock: the assailant is one of us, a fellow Trustee!

I convened a meeting, not in my study as customary, but in the old chapel, with its reminder of the role
of conscience in life. My purpose was to initiate a small
facsimile of trial by jury, every man on his honor. Each
of my six colleagues denied any malfeasance, but no one
more vociferously than our nonagenarian, on whose collar and sleeve I had noticed some minute signs of spatter.
Of course, he replied, what do you expect of a fountain
pen when you inadvertently press too hard on its point?
Why am I alone to be named culpable, when all, except-
ing yourself, write with ordinary pen and ink, as men of
authority usually do? Only you, he went on, conduct

yourself no better than a female office hireling, racketing away into the night.

It was that "female" that was particularly wounding: was it a barb at Miss Margaret Stimmer? Apparently our friendship had escaped not a few. And so, since the others unanimously supported the likely culprit's deflecting hypothesis (and I am sorry to say that further discussion deteriorated into a vigorous comparison of fountain pen brands, whether the Parker is actually superior to the Montblanc, etc.), my effort to secure justice and truth came to nothing.

*

July 12, 1949. I no longer walk in the evenings (and besides, the paths are precariously littered with splintered branches), and have come to a certain understanding with myself. I will not permit the hurtful hostility of others to undermine what moves me. This was a lesson I learned in boyhood, when on account of my growing interest in Ben-Zion Elefantin I too became persona non grata. Our early initiation into a mutual liking of chess was bound to turn public, with my door always open in compliance with Reverend Greenhill's instruction. No wonder our venture took on an aspect of the conspiratorial: whispered notions of when it was best to be free of the herd, or too abruptly quitting the refectory, first one, and then the other. On two or three weekday occasions, as I painfully recall, when we had found refuge in the vacant chapel, we were discovered and mocked, Ben-Zion Elefantin for his name and his incomprehensible origin, and I for my intimacy with so freakish a boy.

I speak too easily of intimacy; it was slow in coming, and was never wholly achieved. He was unnatural in too many ways. The abundance of his uncut hair, for instance: not only its earth-red yet unearthly color, but what I suspected might be a pair of long curls sprouting from the temples, each one hidden behind an ear and lost in the overall mass. Through his shut door (he never obeyed any principle he disliked) I would sometimes hear the rise and fall of foreign mutterings, morning and evening, as if he were quietly growling secret incantations. There were times when, both of us fatigued by too many battles of knights and bishops, he would sit silent and staring, having nothing to say, and waiting for me to signal some subject of merit. I told him of Mr. Canterbury's terrible reign, and how he ought to be glad to have missed it, and of the visit the previous year from Pelham, a nearby town, of an elderly Mr. Emmet, one of the Temple cousins, hence also cousin to Henry James, whose portrait hung in the chapel. To have Mr. Emmet in our midst, however briefly (he spent but an hour or two), was considered a privilege: he had once enjoyed an afternoon's colloquy with Henry James Senior, the novelist's father, when the philosopher Emerson, who happened also to be present, shook Mr. Emmet's hand, and asked him how he was, and made some comment on the charms of Concord, delighting Mr. Emmet with his attentions. For us, we were advised, great fame attached itself to Mr. Emmet's very flesh: his was the hand that the philosopher's hand had honored.

Emmet, Temple, James: all these local references, so dear to the Academy's history, and passed fervently on to its pupils, left Ben-Zion Elefantin indifferent; but the mention of Canterbury roused him in a way I had never before witnessed, and he told me that it was one of the places he had been to school, and where he first learned to read English. Of all languages, he said, the language of English people was his favorite, and though he had been put in school in Canterbury for only a few weeks, and was soon taken away to Frankfurt and afterward Rome, he fell permanently into the sea of their stories, Mary Lamb's Tales from Shakespeare and The Old Curiosity Shop and Ivanhoe and Robinson Crusoe and Adam Bede, books I had barely heard of and would never care to read, as he did, on his own, and have never read since. He told all this as if in confidence, as if he trusted me not to disclose it, as if to disclose it would increase what he believed to be his peril. He seemed to me pitiful then, with his unnatural hair and unnatural voice, which I all at once heard not so much as stilted but as somehow mysteriously archaic, or (I hardly know my own meaning as I tell this) uncannily ancestral. Too many cities were in his tones, and I argued that no one can come from everywhere, everyone must come from somewhere, and where specifically was he from? He thanked me again for our several tournaments and crossed the hall and again shut his door.

I was by now used to such opacities, and scarcely minded them, having other annoyances to trouble me, chiefly my lost status. I was, after all, a Petrie, and a Petrie by nature belongs to the mockers, not to the mocked. I sometimes thought of reversing my lot by joining in the ridicule of Ben-Zion Elefantin; but I quickly learned, after a single attempt, that it could not be done: once an outcast, always an outcast. And more: the humiliation I felt in my inability to recover my standing was small in comparison to the flood of shame that unexpectedly overtook me in having momentarily betrayed Ben-Zion Elefantin. As for the jibes, in time they diminished (I had observed Reverend Greenhill summon the worst of our tormentors for a talk), and in their place we were mutely snubbed like a pair of invisible wraiths. But it freed us from hiding, and since no one would speak to either of us, and Ben-Zion Elefantin had little to say to me, we were anyhow thrown together under a carapace of unwilling quiet. In the refectory I sat close to him with my full dinner plate before me as he carefully drew out the yolk from his single egg. And the same in chapel, when I could sense from my nearness to his breathing how tensely he listened to the readings of Scripture.

On a certain morning of fine weather when Exodus was the theme of Reverend Greenhill's sermon, and the rout of the Egyptians was under moral consideration (whether so massive a drowning of men and horses was too wrathful a punishment even for oppressors), Ben-Zion Elefantin for the first time made himself known to me. A three-hour Sunday afternoon recess had been declared: another of Reverend Greenhill's ameliorating innovations, where formerly Mr. Canterbury had enforced a Sabbath study period of the same length, to be conducted in strictest silence. On this day of freedom, while our classmates were out on the sunny lawns, tossing balls and aimlessly running and blaring their laughter to the skies, Ben-Zion Elefantin and I sat on my bed as usual, with my chessboard between us. But the game was somehow desultory, and on an impulse, remembering the morning's sermon and the strange profundity of his attentiveness, I told him that I owned some actual things from the time of the Pharaohs, whether he could believe me or not. My father, before I was born, I said, was once in Egypt, when my mother was too ill to go with him, but still he brought back for her a gold Egyptian ring, which for some reason she never wore. I said I had often seen the ring in the pretty bowl on her dresser along with her necklaces and bracelets, but it interested me far less than the other things my father had come home with, and if he didn't believe me that they were really from Egypt, I could show them to him. I had never before spoken to anyone of what lay hidden in the pouch in the cabinet under my table, and the reader may question why I did so now. A kind of agitation seemed to possess him, and I saw that his face was burning bloodlike, nearly the color of his hair. You know nothing of Egypt, he said, nothing, you think everything in the Bible is true, but there is more than the Bible tells, and omission is untruth. (I am trying to render the queer way of his speech, how the suddenness of its heat turned it old and ornate, as if he was not a boy but a fiery ghost in some story.) I'll show you, I said, and what makes you think you know more about Egypt than my own father, who really was there, and went down the Nile in a boat, and was close to Sir Flinders Petrie, his cousin, an expert on everything Egyptian, and do you even know who Sir Flinders Petrie is? He said he did not, but neither would Sir Flinders Petrie, whoever he was, know the truth of Ben-Zion Elefantin. This took me aback; how stupid you sound, I said, and he gave me an answer both triumphal, as in an argument he was bound to win, and also despairing, as if he was conscious of how I would receive it. I myself, he said, was born in Egypt, and lived there until it was time for my schooling. I was instantly doubtful: hadn't my father in his notebook described the Egyptians as dusky?

And in pictures of pyramids and palms and such weren't Egyptians always shown to be copper-colored? Certainly no Egyptian had hair the color of red earth. You can't be Egyptian, I said. Oh, he said, I am not Egyptian at all. But if you were born in Egypt and aren't Egyptian, I asked, what are you? Then I saw something like a quiver of fear pass over his eyelids. I am Elefantin, he said, and he

*

July 19, 1949. It has been more than a week since I was made to break off, and I have since not had the heart to come back to my Remington. At that time, as it happened, I had been typing at three in the afternoon, and I hope the reader will not be tempted to think that I had altered my midnight labors out of cowardice, to accommodate my accusers. No, it was because I was driven to go on, my memories racked me, and though three was most often the hour when I helplessly succumbed to a doze, with the fans struggling against the heat, still I could not contain my feeling, stirred as I was by my retelling of Ben-Zion Elefantin's unimaginable words (which I have yet to record). So inwardly gripped was I, that I was altogether deaf to the voices that wafted through the open window, until I was distracted by an unwelcome tumult of loud and offensive laughter. In some exasperation I looked out to see its source. My six colleagues were lazily gathered under the maples, a sign that they were hardly at work on their memoirs. One of them, his arm in the air, appeared to be pointing upward, directly at my window, and then the laughter erupted again. It was, not surprisingly, that childish cackling old man, the spiteful culprit himself, the vandal, the despoiler of my Remington. He stood with his walker before him, and, having caught my eye, stepped forward with the start of a salute, as if about to wave in ill-intended greeting. And then—I knew it seconds before—a broken branch under his feet—he had been looking up and never saw it. He tottered for an instant and lurched downward, his legs snarled in the legs of the walker, and fell in a twisted heap of elderly limbs. I was witness to all of it, the shrieking and calling, Hedda and two or three others of the staff all at once there, warning and herding the others out of the way, five stricken old men, and then the ambulance with its distant siren, and the police and the gurney, and my enemy was taken away. He died in the hospital six days later (yesterday), not, they say, from the fractured hip or the surgery or the infamously inevitable pneumonia that set in soon after, but from, they say, heart failure. And Hedda tells me, with some contempt, that one of the kitchen help believes it was I who destroyed him, I with my evil eye. A foolish superstition, yet I feel its vengeful truth.

We were seven, and now we are six. I think incessantly of death, of oblivion, how nothing lasts, not even memory when the one who remembers is gone. And how can I go on with my memoir, to what end, for what purpose? What meaning can it have, except for its writer? And for him too (I mean for me), the past is mist, its figures and images no better than faded paintings. Where now is Ben-Zion Elefantin, did he in fact exist? Today he is no more than an illusion, and perhaps he was an illusion then?

As for the dead man, I cannot mourn. How can I mourn the envious boor who wounded my sweet Peg? Still, there is a kind of mourning in the air, the gloom seeps and seeps, one feels the breath of a void, not only of a missing tenant of Temple House (him I cannot mourn) but of the limitless void that awaits us. The tremor in my left hand has lately worsened. When I shave, the leathern creature in the mirror is someone I do not know, and too often I draw blood from his living flesh, if flesh it is. Hedda reports that the afternoon tea trays, all save mine, are sent back untouched. And more: she tells me that the other one, that other puerile fellow, the dead man's inseparable accomplice and defender, sits all day in his apartment and weeps. But I cannot forget that when my enemy stood pointing and jeering at my window, the laughter of his steady companion was the loudest. (So much for the delicate syllables of their precious Gerard Manley Hopkins.)

★

July 20, 1949. I have decided, after all, to continue with my memoir. Too many reflections on death contaminate life. And should not each man live every day as if he were immortal? After all this time, I cannot proceed from where I left off: let those broken words hang cryptic and unfinished while I describe my surprise at Ben-Zion Elefantin's indifference to my father's treasure. With the exception of the notebook, I had emptied the pouch of all its objects, one by one, and set them out in a row on my table. I say his indifference, but since his turmoil was unabated, I should rather say contempt. You suppose these things to be uncommon, he said, on account of what you believe to be their ancient age, but your father may have been gullible, as so many are. They can be found by the hundreds, real and false. My parents would know. They know such things with their fingertips. My father, I protested, wasn't gullible, and why should your parents know more than my father, who brought them back from Egypt? My father, I told you, worked in Giza with Sir Flinders Petrie, his very own cousin, and Sir Flinders Petrie isn't gullible, he knows more about Egypt than anyone. He coughed out a small gurgling noise that I took to be a scoff, and then his voice too became small and quiet and more foreign than ever. My parents, he said, are traders.

Even as a boy of ten I understood what a trader was. My father, I had seen, was every morning absorbed by stocks and bonds, and followed them in the newspapers, and besides, according to what I took in from his talk, I knew that traders lived in Wall Street, not in legendary places like Egypt. All this I explained to Ben-Zion Elefantin. And after this conversation he had no more to say, and I was glad that I had not yet revealed to his certain scorn, as I had at first intended, what I imagined to be my father's dearest prize, the emerald-eyed beaker in its box under my bed. A misunderstanding had come between us, or was it a quarrel, and why? He left me and went to his room and again shut the door, and for all the next week he kept away.

*

July 21, 1949. The reader will, I trust, understand why I must eke out my memoir in these unsatisfying patches. In part it is simple fatigue. The tremor in my left hand has somehow begun to assert itself in my right hand as well, hence my typing becomes blighted by too many errors, which I must laboriously correct. After an hour or so at my Remington I feel called upon to lie down, and invariably this leads to a doze. I will confess to another cause of hiatus upon hiatus, and here I admit also to a growing sympathy for my colleagues, who, it is clear, have achieved little or nothing beyond an initial paragraph or two, if even that. As I move on with my chronicle, I more and more feel an irrepressible ache of yearning, I know not for what. Hardly for my boyhood in the Academy, with all its stringencies and youthful cruelties. I am, if I may express it so, in a state of suffering of the soul as I write, a suffering that is more a gnawing paralysis than a conscious pain. I earnestly wish to stop my memoir, and I may not, so how can I blame those others who have stopped, or not so much as begun? I fear that I am again in the grip of the void. All around me the talk is of the accident under the maples, and how it came about, and of broken branches, and the terror of falling. Nor am I immune from that terror, and see anew the wisdom of my having given up my meditative if lonely evening walks in the perilous paths beneath the trees. I think of the loneliness I felt in my childhood, which returns to me now, as if all loneliness, past and present, were one. To be shunned in the company of Ben-Zion Elefantin was painful enough (after all, we had each other), but to endure, all on my own, the snubs and the silences of those persecutors who had once been my peers, was another.

Then how relieved and grateful I was when the following Sunday he came to sit quietly beside me in chapel (where the pew had been spitefully left unoccupied to my right and my left), as if he meant to forgive me for what he deemed to be my fault. And when at last we were set free from the tiresome readings and hymns (the sermon that day was from Matthew), with no discussion of any kind he led me not to my room but to his, and we sat on his bed facing each other as always, though with no chess-board between us, and his door shut as always. His room was nearly identical to mine, the bed as narrow, the walls as bare, the ceiling as stained: a monklike cubicle reminiscent, yes, of a prisoner's cell. Still, a certain surprising difference was instantly noticeable. I kept a stack of books on my table, all of them schoolbooks: my History of the World, my Beginner's Algebra, my (hated) Gallic Wars, and so forth; but here his table was altogether clear of any evidence of schooling, as if he meant to wash away all signs of it, except for a fourth-form Intermediate Arithmetic, with its bruised and faded binding, tossed to the floor among gray clumps of wandering dust. (It was plain that he had chosen not to obey the requirement of cleaning one's own room.)

Yet his table held a panoply of perplexing items: a drawstring sack of some fine material, silk or satin, and next to it a pair of small black cubes, or were they boxes, attached to what appeared to be twin leather leashes, rather like a pony's reins. And lying open beside this eerie contraption, a distinctly foreign-looking book. Its blackened corners were frayed, and an unknown odor drifted faintly from it, like the smell, I imagined, of some forest fungus. I saw that its letters were unrecognizable, and asked whether he could actually read such ugly blotches, and what language was that? He said nothing at first, as if deciding whether to answer, and then shut the book and opened the drawer of his table and carefully deposited it there, meanwhile maneuvering the contraption with its curly reins into its sack before positioning this too, again delicately, into that same hidden place. It is very old, this language, he said finally, and I must now apologize to you. You could not know, he said, how could you know, no one ever knows, they suppose this and that, or they think I speak foolishness, and why should I have expected that you, unlike all others, would understand? His voice shook, and also his hands. Perhaps, he said, it is that I believed you to be my friend, and now I am ashamed. I *am* your friend, I said, and was all at once frightened by my own words, as if I might really be speaking truth. To be the friend of a grotesquerie (this fearsome term comes to me only now) seemed far more dangerous than the boyish pariahship that was already my plight. The peril worsened: he slid off his end of the bed and pulled me down beside him, with his face so close to mine that I could almost see my eyes in the black mirror of his own. I had never before felt the heat of his meager flesh; sitting side by side in the chapel's confining pews, our shoulders in their Academy blazers had never so much as grazed—nor had our knees in our short trousers. And now, the two of us prone on the floor among the nubbles of dust, breathing their spores, I seemed to be breathing his breath. Our bare legs in the twist of my fall had somehow become entangled, and it was as if my skin, or his own, might at any moment catch fire. He spoke with a rhythmic rapidity, almost as if he were reciting, half by rote, some time-encrusted liturgical saga. It had no beginning, it promised no end, it was all fantastical middle, a hallucinatory mixture of languages and implausible histories. And what was I, pressed body to body, to make of it?

The attentive reader (if by now such reader there be) is my witness; only see how I have too long put off the telling of it, and how can I tell it even now, when in fulfillment of my memoir I must? Can I reach out my fingers to capture a cloud, a vapor, an odor? Then do not think that I own the power to replicate any graspable representation of what came to pass that afternoon in my tenth year, when the shouts from the football field were themselves no more than some distant ghostly abrasion. Nevertheless, insofar as my feeble understanding under these circumstances will permit, I will attempt to extract from Ben-Zion Elefantin's untamed babblings a semblance of human coherence. As I say, I must try. But no, it cannot be done; not by me, and who else is there? No other person on earth, and this damnable tremor begins to rock my wrists, my fatigue defeats me, the keys of my Remington are no better than boulders, I fear a panic will soon overtake me if I do not stop, and here thank God is Hedda with the supper tray thank God thank God thank God

3:30 AM

Sleep has eluded me for many hours, so deep is my abashment. To have lost self-possession, and to such a degree, in the presence of the kitchen help! And that Hedda should have seen me so disheveled, with my shirt collar wet, and these shaming infantile tears, how am I different from that forsaken miscreant whom in my private mind I call the Childish One? What is it to me that he mourns his misbegotten accomplice? And what is it Hedda must think? Two old men weeping, two old men grieving? I myself hardly know why I grieve, and for whom? For my unhappy boyhood, for my sweet Peg, for my unlucky and frivolous son? And to find me so undone, and yet to have come with her own lament! Two of the staff have departed, she told me, without a word of warning, and how was she to cope, she and that slattern Amelia, das Flittchen, only the two of them, diese Schlümpfe lazy and useless, left in charge of six broken old men, each more zerbrechlich than the next, the frailest of all starving himself night and day on his dirty sofa with his head down, refusing to eat a crumb of bread or sip a drop of tea, a sick man who ought to be in the hospital? And who was to get him there? Did he have a wife, a daughter, a son? What was she to do with him? What was I, in my capacity as Trustee, to do with him, has he no family, no friend, no heir?

I replied that I would review the Charter of the Trust to determine a suitable course, and then, unable to look her in the eye, I dismissed her.

★

July 22, 1949. Further to the Charter. The original, of course, is in the Academy vault at J. P. Morgan, but I retain a copy here in my study, where I keep it together with my personal volume of the History, though I have rarely consulted it since the establishment of Temple House, when additional clauses were necessarily incorporated. And indeed there is provision for such a contingency as care for the seriously moribund, the funding for which to come under the bank's jurisdiction. Setting all this in motion, alas, falls to me. It cannot escape my judgment that this childless miscreant's predicament is no better than that of a vagrant found dying in the street; yet I who have a son, will my own fate differ when I too inevitably succumb?

It has now been several weeks, in fact I count two months, since I have had any word from my son. In light of the length of this period of silence, I will confess to having broken a wary and unacknowledged vow (unacknowledged by him, wary on my side). I mean by this that rather than wait for his own action in this respect, I undertook to telephone him, in part because I believe his resources are, as usual, low, and in the hope of sparing him the expense of a long-distance call. The result was unfortunate, and I am largely, if unintentionally, to blame. Though I have not spoken of it outright, I presume it is fully evident that given my retirement, and with no further Petrie to carry the firm on into the future (my son having preferred a less onerous path), the venerable Petrie partnership is now lamentably defunct. On this occasion, despite my long-held familiarity with time-zone vagaries—a mere one-hour difference from Chicago, three from Los Angeles, and what law office can function without such instinctive knowledge—my memory abandoned me and caused an unforgivable intrusion: I reached my son in the middle of his California night. He was, I admit, startled, and reminded me that this unexpected disruption was not my first such malfeasance; it had happened twice before. I felt constrained to apologize, which only brought on a kind of confusion, or rather anger, on his part: he explained that he and a collaborator were working through the night on content (his strange jargon) which may have already interested a producer. I believe this is what he told me. Or was it that the producer was at that very moment at his side? Certainly he was not alone; I heard what I took to be a nearby voice, a murmur that was kin to laughter.

These increasing forgettings greatly distress me, and perhaps the ingenious inventors of our modern era, who have already brought us the television sets that are beginning to proliferate even beyond the barroom, will one day devise a telephone that allows one to know the identity of the caller before responding. Such a development would surely inhibit my son's growing coolness, and my embarrassment at discovering him in flagrante delicto.

*

July 25, 1949. What has become of me? Excess emotion has made me shameless, and my tongue (I mean my prose) is paralyzed by coarse legalisms. A memoir ought not to be a deposition, and how I wish it were, with all its conciseness and clarity. Instead, I write, indeed I speak, in turbulence, captive of these helpless tears that terrify me, as if I am already blundering in the haze and corrosions of a dying brain. Was it some crackpot seizure of dream and dementia that took hold of me four days ago when I *could not* summon Ben-Zion Elefantin's deposition, if that is what he meant it to be, his pleading a case for his curious existence, his pitiful defense? How can I find my way out of this wilderness of hesitation? Or dare I say shame?

. . .

5:21 AM. Dawn. My wrists, my very ribs, ache from the keys. Longhand no better. A spilled vessel. Drowned. As if strangled by trance. The voice is not mine. Then whose? And how?

★

July 26, 1949. Here I must explain a change I am introducing in the organization of the admittedly chaotic document presently under my hand. It will be recalled that as these pages accumulated, I at one time stored them in a rectangular box (it once sheltered my father's substantial Cuban cigars) with an ornamental lid, the lid to serve as a warning to trespassers. But the growing length of my memoir can no longer be contained in so shallow a receptacle, and in any event I no longer fear a recurrence of vandalism: the vandal is dead. (Sans gravestone, it pleases me to say. Through Hedda I learn that the nonagenarian's younger brother, himself a fading octogenarian, has disposed of the ashes in some obscure upstate waterway.) Hence I am free now to allow these increasing pages to build as they will, open to sight and secured by a cherished paperweight: my grandfather's antiquated brass notary seal. The vacant box will henceforth have another use. I intend to sequester therein a certain portion of this manuscript, i.e., what I can only describe as my attempt to transcribe the tenor of Ben-Zion Elefantin's utterances. Not, let it be understood, that they have faded over the last seven or more decades. On the contrary: they remain for me akin to a burning bush, unquenchable. I will determine later whether I judge this putative transcription to be suitable or worthy (I mean comprehensible). If not, and it is the crux of my memoir, then all that I have set down so far will be null and void. But even if it should have a certain validity, ought it to be preserved? Or does it demand to be hidden, lest it expose an already broken being, one whom I once loved (while unaware of that love) and whose whereabouts today I do not know?

*

[Note: concealed herein are the papers in question. As of this writing, August 2, 1949, they will so remain until their disposition is determined, which determination will itself depend on the trustworthiness of the contents.]

You asked how I came here to the Academy. My uncle brought me. In every city where my parents are obliged to leave me, there is always an uncle to choose a school for me, yet not one of them is truly an uncle. How my present uncle happened on this place, it is impossible to surmise. It may be that he was impressed by what he took to be a congenial name, and believed that my parents might be pleased by it. My father and mother are transients and travelers, with no settled home, they are buyers and sellers, they are seekers and doubters, and they live mainly in hotels. Some of these hotels are pleasant, most are not, but rather than being shut up in a school, I always prefer those indifferent rooms where we never stay long and I am never expected to explain who I am, or pressed to find a friend my own age. When I was much younger, I pleaded to be taken wherever they might go, and promised that I would never complain of the heat or cry if I hated the food, and would never be sick, and would always be good. But they told me there were too many dangers for a child in those Levantine regions of constant upheaval where their particular business led them. To calm me, they explained as simply as they could that though they held themselves out to be ordinary traders, they were in truth pilgrims in search of a certain relic of our heritage, and that this was the primary hope of their work. Somewhere, I came to understand, lying unrecognized in one of the thousand alleyways and souks in the village markets of Egypt, or Palestine, or Syria, or Iraq, this significant thing, whatever it was, could be uncovered.

And when I asked why it was significant, they assured me that one day, when I was older, I would see for myself, and meanwhile, until it was found, they must earn our bread. This, they said, was the reason for their peregrinations: it was for the sake of foreign objects, exceedingly ancient, that persons in the West coveted and might wish to buy. And when I asked why these objects were coveted, my father replied It is for the vanity of the coveters, and my mother said It is because they are hollow and have no histories of their own. This was the cause of our having come to New York, where there are many such buyers. Our hotel in this city was too small and too cramped and too noisy, near streets made too bright in the middle of the night and crowds swimming like fishes all around, but still I would be more content to be left in such an unsavory scene than confined here where there are grasses and trees and schoolbooks without interest or weight, and where Scripture, the story of my people, is derided and whistled at by unlettered boys. My parents are not to blame, they must leave me behind to purchase their wares from fellahin who scratch with their hoes among the stones of the field, or from hawkers who crook their fingers under the shadowy arches of defeated cities. And soon an uncle will come to take me away to another hotel in another country, where a different uncle will accompany me to another school.

What my parents promised has come to pass. Though the significant thing has yet to be discovered, I have by now seen for myself who we are. My family name reveals our origins, which for reasons of rivalry and obfuscation have been omitted from the Books of the Jews, where it ought by historic rights to have been set within the chronicles of the Israelites. Never mind that there are in our own language missives attesting to our presence—we Elefantins remain outcasts from the history of our people. They say of us that because of our far-flung island home we were without knowledge of the breadth of the imperatives of Moshe our Teacher, whom we revered, and followed into the wilderness. As if we are not ourselves Israelites, as if we too did not stand at Sinai among the multitudes of the Exodus! If it is true that we have been erased from Torah, it is because we are victims of falsifying scholars, betrayers who have become our interpreters. They have written of us as servile mercenaries, willing sentries for the haughty Persians who overran Egypt and commanded a fort to fend off yet other invaders—but are they not themselves mercenaries in the pay of the lies of the scholars? We, the Elefantins, hold our own truths. Our traditions and practices are far weightier than the speculations of those ignorant excavators, those papyrologists who pollute our ruined haven with their inventions and prevarications. Of our truth they make legends. Hirelings on behalf of the Persian conquerors of Egypt we never were! With our generations of loam-red hair, Nubians and Egyptians we are not. Rather we are what our memories tell us, lost stragglers, dissenters who became separated in the wilderness from that mixed throng of snivelers after the fleshpots of our persecutors. We alone were unyieldingly faithful to Moshe our Teacher, we alone never succumbed to their foolish obeisance to a gilded bovine of the barnyard. Willingly we parted from them, and blundered our way we knew not where, and in the scalding winds of the desert hardly discerned north from south, or east from west. In the innocent blindness of our flight we turned back to an Egypt ruled now not by pharaohs but by foreign overlords, a green island inhabited by idolators who there had built a temple to Khnum, a fantastical god of the Nile in the ludicrous shape of a ram, and yet another god with the limbs of a man and the head of a stork, and still other gods of the river, red-legged storks that they mummified to preserve their divinity. And for their rites and libations they fashioned slender vessels made in the image of storks. All the gods of the nations are ludicrous, and all are fantastical, all but the Creator of All who created all the suns and their planets, and all the rivers and seas of the earth. And because we had no fear of the imaginings they called their gods, who for lack of existence could not have ordered the fullness and withdrawal of the Nile, we built, very near to their fraudulent shrine, our Temple to the Creator of All. It was in this way that we came as true Israelites to Elephantine.

These were the beliefs and writings and precepts of the heritage I received from my father and my mother, who had received the very same from their predecessors, as they in turn had received them from our distant progenitors who raised up the Temple at Elephantine. Since then, we have been as a people scattered and few, and worse: forgotten, as if we never were. We live on as if in hiding. Even when our Temple stood, how humble it was, and how it disdained grandeur! It was built low to the earth, and constructed of earth, with a modest courtyard and fine tiles on its floor, and never a pillar blooming with crests of stone flora. We were, after all, stragglers. It was not our fate to go up to Jerusalem, or to set eyes on the stream that is called Jordan. Our companionate river was the Nile, once divinely bloodied so that we as a wretched people could escape our condition as slaves. It was through our proximity to the watery site of these memories that the Passover remains precious to us—and still we are expelled from the Books of the Jews!

And then, in a turn of our fortune, it was revealed to us by certain travelers that on a summit in the town of Jerusalem there was still another Temple, this one very grand, and peopled by Priests and Levites, to whom letters were sent, and from whom letters arrived. They too spoke and wrote our language, as who among the nations did not? In their inquiries we saw that though we may have been acknowledged as fellow Israelites, we were also regarded as improbable curiosities: they wished to know how we lived, how our families and neighbors were constituted, what our usages were, what plants and beasts and fowl there were on our island, and much else. We told them of the rich moisture of our

reddish clay, how sheep and cattle were few while birds
were many, especially the storks that thrived in colonies
in the shallows of the Nile; and at first they made no
murmurings against our Temple. And little by little,
as we informed them of our beginnings and our ways,
we learned theirs: the history of how their Temple was
ruined, and how they were exiled to Babylon, and how
they returned to rebuild it, all under the rule of the very
Persians for whom we were supposedly abject hirelings!
They told us of their commandments and ordinances,
written in the books we stragglers did not possess,
they told us of the Book of their teachers Ezra and
Nehemiah, and their Book of holy instructions called
Dvarim. And according to the wisdom of these books,
they believed that only their Temple on the heights
of Jerusalem permitted worship of the Creator of All,
and that all other sanctums were forbidden, inclined as
they were to the ludicrous and fantastical gods of the
nations, and to false icons of gold and licentious figurines. And so it was according to the wisdom of these
books that our riverine Temple, so contagiously close
to the delusionary shrine of Khnum, was soon deemed
illicit. But was not our Temple, like theirs, adorned
by a seven-branched menorah, and a shulchan for the
shewbread, and did not our kohanim, like theirs, honor
the rites of sacrifice, were not birds brought by our
people as burnt-offerings, all the birds that were pure,

and none, like the stork, that were not? And was not our Temple also razed by enemies, our neighbors the priests of Khnum, who hated us because we doubted their gods? And were we too not exiled from our soil and compelled to sojourn elsewhere? We who revered Moshe our Teacher and faithfully followed him into the wilderness and never made obeisance to a gilded bovine of the barnyard!

It is through these commandments and ordinances that we have been made to disappear. And so we live on as apparitions, fearful of mockery. And I, Ben-Zion Elefantin, am just such an apparition, am I not?

*

August 3, 1949. Oh my feelings, my feelings! How they drive me, not since the passing of my darling, my Peg, my own sweet Peg, never since then, and I scarcely know why. My father's box here on my desk a veritable oven, the words within burn and burn, indeed they smell of clinging smoke, I begin to fear they are counterfeit, contraband of my own making, my brain is dizzied, I am not myself, we are under a violent tropical heat breathing fire, 103 degrees on this the second brutal day of it, the fans vanquished, a cosmic furnace where sanity wants nothing more than ice water, and this foolish woman chooses to cook her Saftgoulasch! She comes to me panting, with a red face and the sweat flooding her neck, to give me news of that feckless pair of kitchen defectors, and to complain yet again how doubly hard the work is for her without the men to do the heavy labor, is she expected to lift barrels? And das Flittchen Amelia, she is for spite schtum (when excited Hedda loses hold of her English), she knows three days already where they go, ein hochnäsige restaurant making bigger its business where are so many trains and in this bitter house so much work and Mäuse in the pantry and that old man sick in his head crying crying stinking of his own kacken, wie lang müssen wir noch auf diese verehrte Finanziere und ihre blöden Papiere warten?

And so forth. I told her that the mills of the bankers grind slowly, and what leads her to think that in such miserable heat any normal man could get that greasy damn stew down his gullet, and as for the mainstay of the staff going off to wait tables in the city, no wonder the rats are leaving the sinking ship, so why not the Oyster Bar in preference to this waning mice-ridden edifice?

Hedda is a respectable woman. I have never before quarreled with her. I have never thought to offend her.

*

August 5, 1949. Relief. After four detestable days, that hellish heat wave has broken. Hedda has begun to speak to me again, though I never did eat her stew. As for the Oyster

Bar's coming to mind, I believe it must have been some considerable time before my retirement that Ned Greenhill and I last lunched there. It was convenient for both of us, my office just around the corner from Grand Central, and the Courthouse downtown, ten minutes by subway. In homage to the name, Ned habitually ordered oysters, while I, mindful of my nervous digestion, kept to milder flounder. The place in those days had its own confidential dimness. A couple of fellows could sit with their drinks in a semblance of seclusion, while up and down the ramp the plebs ran for their trains. I remember how the tables vibrated with the underground scrapings of wheels on rails. A pity, all this remodeling and refurbishing and hiring of new staff. Nowadays every comfortable old space submits to this fad of architectural vastness, every public room a modernist boast. Happily the Academy escaped this destiny when it was metamorphosed into Temple House, though perhaps too many of the original Oxonian genuflections were retained. (I mean those fortresslike gray turrets that some of the upper-form rowdies claimed were in need of condoms.) Casual reminiscences such as these began our infrequent meetings, but after several glasses of wine we ventured, on the occasion I allude to, into more personal exchanges. I might insert here that Ned is careful never to speak of his son, I suspect out of consideration of me, since I have so little to say of mine. Unlike many of his kind, he is no braggart, especially in view of his own success. (I see in the Times that he is currently being sought after for an appellate appointment.) At Harvard he studied philosophy with one Harry Wolfson, a luminary unfamiliar to me, but well known, Ned made clear, to Reverend Greenhill—at least to his library, as I lately saw for myself. (I regret to say that I also saw rodent droppings all along the shelves.) Ned's memories of our long-ago headmaster have often dominated our conversations: Reverend Greenhill's amusement at the similarity of their family names coexisting with the dissimilarity of their ancestry, his eagerness to introduce Ned to the understanding of Greek, and his general favoritism toward Ned, unluckily making him the butt of his classmates.

At his mention of this word, I asked whether he recalled an undersized and taciturn fourth-form boy with a farcical pachyderm name, which everyone ridiculed. I said this jokingly, and almost dismissively, so as not to reveal my ardent interest in what he might tell me. Oh yes, he said, who could forget such an oddity, myself in particular, since I too was mocked, and worse than mocked, along with the other Jewish boys, but in my case all the more so because Reverend Greenhill had singled me out. It was not only for the pleasure he took in my being drawn to the classical languages, rare enough in the Academy, he told me, but also because he had observed my restraint when bullied, and believed I might understand this boy's irregular situation, and would be willing to befriend him. No former headmaster had agreed to take in a pupil sent over from the Elijah Foundation, and Canterbury his predecessor had insisted on its improbability on grounds of proper religion. I was curious to know what was the nature of such a Foundation? No one today, he said, speaks of orphans and orphanages, these terms are thankfully obsolete, but one can only suppose that a circumstance of this kind might account for the peculiarity of so untypical a boy. When I learned that at the Foundation the chief praisesong of their worship is cantillated in the language spoken by Our Lord, I invited him to have the run of my library, where he might find volumes of theological and historical appeal. He brightened at this, but only fleetingly. Unhappily his diffidence was such that he shrank from entering my study. Yet what Reverend Greenhill asked of me, Ned said, was impossible. To be seen in the company of a leper with a leper's name? I was myself too much the target of nasty cracks.

In Ned's tone, I should add, there was nothing of complaint or grievance. He spoke with simple matter-of-factness, whether improvised or not. And somehow I could not resist asking if he recalled that it was I who had dared to befriend Ben-Zion Elefantin: did he remember that? Oh, he said, passing your open door on my way for my hour with Reverend Greenhill, I once saw the two of you bent over some sort of board game, and of course like everyone else I knew the rowdies had you in their sights, as they had me, but I put it out of my mind. The truth is it gave me a twinge of guilt. I did badly that day with my Xenophon.

After this, I turned rather self-consciously away from this subject to a blander one, and when we shook hands and parted and I was back in my office, I requested one of the clerks to look up a certain Elijah Foundation and make a note of the results. In the end he found nothing; such an entity no longer exists, and why should it, after so many decades? And why is it plausible that Ned Greenhill's recollection of words uttered a lifetime ago to a vulnerable child of ten should hold water? And besides, is it not likely that it was a different boy Reverend Greenhill spoke of all those years before? And not Ben-Zion Elefantin?

But for the rest of that day I was unaccountably thrown into an unusual dejection, and if not for the kind concern of my own good Peg (Miss Margaret Stimmer as she was then), I might not have recovered my spirits. Nor have I since met with Ned Greenhill.

★

August 9, 1949. For the last several hours I have been ruminating over what I have come more and more to think of as Ben-Zion Elefantin's entreaty. How fragile it is, and yet how persuasive! My transcription, so called, of Ben-Zion Elefantin's history continues to occupy my father's cigar box, forbidden to any eye but my own. It will be plain to the excluded reader that here he will find himself at a disadvantage. And for good reason: my growing apprehension. Is Ben-Zion Elefantin's testimony, if I may take it to be that, a wizardly act of my own deceit? His pleadings are the very marrow, and may I say the soul, of my memoir, and when I lift them out of their shelter (as I must shamelessly admit I am too often tempted to do) I am made heartsick, as by the hovering of a revenant. And sometimes, in these sluggish midafternoons when I am seized by an overpowering stupor, I seem to see my father's cigar box elide into the pretty china dish where my mother kept the scarab ring she never wore.

*

August 13, 1949. Hideous. Horrible and hideous. I cannot cleanse my eyes of it. Hedda's shriek, and then Amelia running through the corridors shouting for me to come, come, come! That thing, barely a man, dangling in the night from the lit chandelier with its head horribly loosened, the tongue bulging, the necktie and its yellow butterflies twisted tight around the throat, the glass beads and teardrops swaying and tinkling like harps

*

August 14, 1949. At three o'clock this afternoon, mindful of the time gap, I telephoned my son. Noon in Los Angeles. He was still asleep, I could not help myself, I have no one dear to me, how alone I am, I feel strangled by my own vagrant fears. I despised this man, I thought him infantile in his attachment, the close companion of a vandal, if not himself a vandal, the two of them a cabal of criminality. But to take his own life because he could not bear the grieving, what am I to make of this? My son is indifferent to all of it, the suicide of a stranger, but what of my own hurt, how can he not see it, the fickleness of life, the cryptic trail of the past (my father's desertion of my mother), and what of his own futility? I often feel that my son grudges me his time, yet today he took me by surprise, showing no impatience, assuring me there was no intrusion and that anyhow he had lately been sleeping lightly, buoyed up by what was almost certain to become his breakthrough, and do I know who William Wyler is? Wyler himself, he said, not his assistant, promises to get to my treatment early next week, likes the basic idea, seems excited by it, and so forth and so on, and how many times have I been apprised of this mirage by my deluded son? The oasis is always over the next hill. And the next hill is always more of the same desert.

I am not a jealous man. As a person of lineage, and as the heir and partner of a highly reputable law firm, I have never had a reason to envy. Rather, throughout my career, others have envied me. My father, had he lived to know of it, would have been pleased by at least the outward course of my life, my early achievements (e.g., editor in chief, Yale Law Journal), my marriage into a family similar in standing to our own, and whatever considerable esteem I have earned in the civic area. Despite the recklessness of his youth, my father was for the entirety of his remaining days a wholly conventional man, with conventional expectations. I believe I have met them. That my son has not met mine is a lasting and festering bruise. Every month or so I read of yet another landmark acquisition by Edwin Jacobs Greenhill, Jr., the most recent being the Algonquin, a hotel famous thirty years ago for its literary cachet, and by my count his fourth such midtown purchase.

Ned, I am aware, has grandchildren. My son is two years older than Ned's. Both are middle-aged men. Can a treatment, so called, be said to possess literary cachet?

And I cannot, cannot, cannot cleanse my eyes of that horrific hanging thing.

*

August 19, 1949. Hedda has come to me with a substantial bundle of clothing, all of finest quality, just look here the linings and here also the stitches, and so many rich ties, this poor sickinthehead Mann dünn wie eine Krähe im Winter, she is sending these nice things to a charity, would I like to keep two or three of the neckties?

I told her I would not.

In describing my father as conventional some days ago, I meant it as a praiseworthy trait, perhaps as much for myself as for him. But nothing of that can be true. My God, how I falsify! There were certain times in my childhood, well before I was sent to the Academy, and when my mother was preoccupied elsewhere (she often spent evenings at one or another event at her Women's Club), I would see my father settle into a chair in his study with his newspaper, and angrily toss it away, and sit and stare at the glass door of the cabinet that held his collection. For long minutes he would open that door and stare, or he would stare through the glass with the door shut. He never took out any of these objects. I was always a little afraid of him during these motionless scenes, when he seemed as wooden and lifeless as one of my toy soldiers. I would be crouched on the carpet nearby watching for his breath to resume, hoping my mother would come home and this silent and wooden starer would turn back into the father I knew.

It is because of these distant impressions that now and then assault me in unheralded snatches of panic that I believe my father harbored somewhere in his ribs an untamed creature. Unlike him, I am no dissembler, I am subject to no fantastic imaginings. And yet I feel all at sea, my memoir is of no more import than some wild pestilential growth, and what idiocy it was to think that it could be chained, as originally proposed, by ten typewritten sheets!

*

September 2, 1949. 4 PM. It is now nearly two weeks since with some urgency I advised Mr. John Theory, my current liaison at Morgan, of the need for the transfer of one of the Trustees here to a nursing facility. This morning there came from him what I expected to be confirmation, however delayed, of the completed arrangements, while meanwhile the disrepute brought upon this house by the disgrace of suicide has erased all such necessity; so it may be that what is merely moot is finally the father of the ironical. I have since learned that John's communication, disturbing in the extreme, has been received by all five remaining Trustees. We are informed that the present situation at Temple House has long been unsustainable, that after private surveillance by the bank it was determined that the physical and financial condition of the premises continues to deteriorate (vermin, easy access by intruders, insufficient outdoors safety for the residents, understaffing, fragile old books a flammable hazard in the kitchen area, etc.), that the ill-considered renovations of so many years ago are inappropriate for the residents (dangerously weighty ceiling lighting fixtures, the attractive nuisance of a dimly lit chapel no longer in use), and so forth. In brief: we are required to vacate Temple House by no later than December 15, 1949.

By this hour (7:30 PM) the letters have been read in, it must be said, a flurry of consternation. My colleagues, uninvited, invaded my study shortly after the lunch trays were removed (Hedda has not yet been told of this new calamity), chiefly to bemoan the disruption, as if I, because of my prior interaction with John Theory, were the cause of it. Once again I find I am accused, not surprisingly by one of my earlier accusers, the nonentity who came together with that pernicious twosome to charge me with disturbing the peace. I will not forget that ignominious hammer and tongs, his sole utterance, nor will I give his name. Let him and the others be expunged from my consciousness.

Note how consistent I have been in omitting all names but that of Ned Greenhill, of whom I suspect no ill intent. (For obvious reasons, he was never regarded as eligible to serve as Trustee, yet to this day he has never shown resentment or rancor.) My honorable colleagues, it goes without saying, spare no opportunity to denigrate me. I blame this on that insidious Amelia, who coming one evening to pick up my dinner tray (once again that vile stew), observed me in an idle moment of contemplation.

Randomly dispersed on my table, close to my father's cigar box (with its hidden burden), were a few of his cherished arcana. I say randomly; I should perhaps say dreamily, as when some unforgotten presence presses as palpably as if it were as near and true as living pulse. It seemed to me that I was again on the floor with my wooden brigade, my father was again staring through the glass door, while meanwhile in the cup of my hand lay the bulbous female contours of one of those grotesque figurines, no more than three inches in height, that are prominent among his findings. And here was Amelia spewing out her lascivious giggle and going off, as I soon understood, to spread an infamous aspersion: that I am in the grip of an obscene habit of some kind. Since then, I have been subject to muted but sly hints and taunts, implying that I am given to caress the stone breasts and vulvae of these innocent objects. My worthy peers, elderly widowers all, display the spiteful conduct of a pack of kindergartners!

Hedda herself often remarks on these juvenile provocations in similar vein, having, as she recently confided, until 1932 taught at Vienna's most respected fortschrittliche Grundschule. I think of her as a mundane intelligence, and never presumed she could be formally equipped with what she calls a Masterstudium. And with her dark looks she is certainly not a native Austrian. I have so far had little interest in her bizarre wanderings, though it bemuses me to learn that she was obliged to spend years in some woebegone Caribbean village, where, she insists, the thuggish Trujillo was more open to persons like herself than the American president. (Miranda and I, to tell the truth, naturally cast our votes four times against Roosevelt's socialist schemes, even as we were compelled to overcome our dislike of that near-socialist Wendell Willkie.)

But already today the plans for decampment have begun. The Trustees, to say it outright, are wealthy men: relocation ought not to be a difficulty. But where is one to go?

⋆

September 3, 1949. When this morning I was finally able to reach John Theory (he is rarely at his desk), he replied with a disconcerting testiness, though his telephone manner has in the past never been anything but respectful. Three generations of Petries, I told him, have been with Morgan, and out of the blue you have the gall to put me out on the street? Now listen to me, Lloyd, he said, there is nothing sudden or abrupt here, three months ago I sent you, I mean you personally as designated spokesman for the residents of Temple House, to which position you will recall you readily agreed some four years ago, an official notice stating that an investigation of the condition of the property was soon to begin. You cannot claim, he said, to be surprised. I am acutely surprised, I said, and as for the safety of our environment here, ought that not to be the Trustees' own consideration without extraneous intrusion? Read the Charter, Lloyd, he said (with a good deal of asperity), why don't you just read the Charter, and in fact I returned to it some twenty minutes ago and to my embarrassment located the clause in question. On its face it appears to contradict the earlier in-perpetuity clause, but on further examination I see that some clever Shylock's statutory legerdemain obviates this conflict.

More to the point, I have also found the letter of prior notification John speaks of. It troubles me that I had entirely forgotten it. I believe it must be my immersion in my memoir at the time of its arrival that distracted me, but what is still more vexing is that I discovered this letter in my father's cigar box interleaved among the transcription papers, and have no memory of inserting it there. What could I have been thinking, or was I thinking at all? I have never been subject to carelessness, and surely not to willful negligence. Nevertheless it does not escape me that this new crop of rash young bankers is wanting in both decorum and deference.

*

September 5, 1949. Labor Day. Apparently hoping to compensate for Amelia's recent barbarism, Hedda has come with a page torn out from Life magazine: a large photo of Sigmund Freud's desk in his Vienna study. Parading over its surface are innumerable antiquities similar to my father's, though certainly surpassing his in quantity. See now, Hedda said, one of the greatest thinkers of the century, and no one dares to accuse such a man of Lüsternheit! Clearly she means to flatter (or is it comfort?) me, as if I ought to be impressed by a comparison with this charlatan Jew and his preposterous notions. It can easily be seen throughout my memoir that I have no regard for such absurd posturings; it is the conscious mind I value, not its allegedly secret underworld. So here is this ragged bit of paper (she leaves it on my table and runs off), with all these phantasmagoric pharaonic remnants, bellies and horns, faceless heads, and why do these unfathomable things lead me to remember the heat of Ben-Zion Elefantin's bony shins against my own?

*

September 18, 1949. An unexpected public affliction, this buzzing and swarming of sons and sons-in-law and daughters and daughters-in-law and grandsons and granddaughters, and who knows whatever other likely kin never before known to have been seen on these premises, soon to be razed and replaced by what faddish excrescence? I continue to follow in the Times how that predatory clique of New York developers are sniffing opportunities here in Westchester, with Temple House and its considerable grounds as prime prey. Undoubtedly the maples will give way to asphalt, though today they are all gold, gold at their crowns, gold on the paths, gold gilding the old benches. Our last fall here. The fall of Temple House. And the visitors, the half-forgotten relations, the would-be heirs and successors, coming, as they say, to the rescue, the plans for departure, the summonings, the offerings, the temptings, the resolutions, the invitations, the reassurances: this unwonted outbreak of the fevers of hospitality. Old men's bones will be ash before long; inconceivable that wealthy old men should languish unhoused.

As for me, with no eruption of daughter-in-law or grandchild or so much as a willing cousin (the latter-day Petries and Wilkinsons have hardly been fruitful), yet I too have a son, have I not? Some days ago I informed him of our enforced exodus. He did not beseech me to fly at once to Los Angeles for a new life in the California sunshine. Oh Dad, he said, you know you wouldn't fit in here, it's not your milieu, you wouldn't be happy, and anyhow it's not a generational thing, it's a personality difference: and more demurrals on the same theme. He claims to be studying a freeing philosophy, Oriental in origin, called Zen, as well as the writings of one Martin Buber. (All this astonished me. I am alarmed by these inconstant dilettantisms.) I explained that to lighten the burden of my imminent move, I am about to dispose of much of my material possessions, as well as of certain keepsakes, one of which he had at one time expressed a strong desire to get hold of. I regret my untoward obstinacy in refusing you, I told him, and would be glad to assist in whatever motion picture project you are currently engaged in. I speak not only of financing, though we can surely discuss such an eventuality. Are you, I asked, still interested in making some use of my father's notes on his Egyptian travels, and his inscrutable desertion of my mother, and his unusual friendship with Sir Flinders Petrie? Oh no Dad, he said, it's past time for that sort of thing, not another one of these Near Eastern Westerns with the weeping abandoned bride, thanks all the same. And he made no further mention of William Wyler.

There is no way I can win back my son: not by bribery, not by appeasement. Not by a love I cannot feel. I have loved only twice. Once my glorious Peg. And once, long ago, Ben-Zion Elefantin.

*

September 22, 1949. How many hours we lay there entwined I cannot say, nor can I recall whether either of us had surrendered, as I now suppose, to what must have been a kind of half-sleep. For myself, I know that the sun crept from one corner of the ceiling to another, and that I tracked its slow progress with indolent eyes. Nor can I say that

I was fully awake, though the murmurings that swirled around me were remnants of Ben-Zion Elefantin's small low catlike growlings, rising and ebbing, so that here and there I took him to be invoking a foreign tongue, even as I apprehended his meaning. By now the far-off football shouts had diminished, and a commotion in the corridors signaled that the dinner hour had arrived, and that our classmates had begun their raucous rush to the refectory. This reminded me that I was parched; my palate was no better than a dry ribbed plain, and while Ben-Zion Elefantin, with his curious patience, peeled away the shell of his boiled egg, I drank innumerable cups of water, as if my thirst could consume some bottomless Niagara. I had no hunger at all. We sat, he and I, in a quiet made more dense by the clamor all around, and said nothing, until he pushed his chair back from the table and left me. This time I did not follow.

If only lost minutes could be reconstructed (minutes, I mean, in a boy's mind seventy years ago), I would today perhaps understand what I understood only faintly then. He was throwing me off, he had no wish for me to pursue him. Something there was in me that had made him ashamed. It was my pity he felt; he recoiled from it. Pity, he knew, was no more than blatant disbelief. Or else it was belief: that I thought him crazed. It may be that I did think him crazed, as a fabricator is crazed by the dazzle of his fabrication. And indeed I was dazzled, as I am even now, by the ingenuity of his fable, if that is what it was, and by the labyrinth of his boyish brain. And by the piteous loneliness of his thin legs. He had abandoned me once before, when I had misunderstood his words; but his words were like no other boy's words, so how was I to blame? And am I not myself the son of a crazed father, so how am I to blame?

The reader will conclude that I am mistaking pity for love.

Conclude however you please.

And for a second time (this was in chapel the next morning, when Reverend Greenhill's text was Jonah's refusal to preach to Nineveh), I saw yet again how humbly Ben-Zion Elefantin could sink into his shoulder blades as if to hide from himself. I am sorry, he said, that I made you so thirsty. You didn't make me thirsty, I said, I just was. But I did make you thirsty, he said. Look, I said, come to my room at recess, there's something I want to show you. I never want anyone else to see it, you're the only one. All right, he said, I will come. Or maybe, I said, I'll bring it to your room because you always keep your door shut. And then Reverend Greenhill began to describe the big fish, which he explained wasn't necessarily an actual whale, and to my surprise I found myself listening with some interest.

★

September 24, 1949. It was on this day seven years ago that my poor Peg passed on. I have visited her burial site only on three particular occasions (I think of these as our small private anniversaries), and never since the last. Like me, she had no siblings, and her parents were long gone, so it was I who arranged for her spare marble gravestone in St. Mark's Episcopal Cemetery, a short drive not far from Temple House. (Her origins were midwest Methodist, but no matter.) I had intended to go there often, to reflect on the words I had myself composed: Margaret Gertrude Stimmer, A Companion Valorous and Pure. I had hoped that this would give me if not consolation, then the will to bear her absence; yet before long I learned to my chagrin that my repeated presence there provoked unpleasant gossip among my colleagues. (My own interment, as is fitting, will be beside Miranda in the Petrie family plot.)

*

September 25, 1949. Once again the anxieties of my present musings disrupt my focus and send my thoughts flying: what am I to do with my father's things, where am I to go, and will I be compelled to jettison my Remington? Even so, these insecurities must not sway me from the urgency of my purpose. Then let it be noted that in the very hour of my assignation with Ben-Zion Elefantin, recess was suspended. Instead, Forms Four through Eight were required to attend a lecture, to be held in the refectory, by a respected acquaintance of Reverend Greenhill's, whose name has disappeared from my memory, though I can still see his thin pale fingers fluttering over the buttons of his vest as if in a failing plea for our unruly attention. Gentlemen, Reverend Greenhill began (he addressed us thus in the aggregate, though otherwise he called each boy by his family name), our subject today, however geographically distant, transpires, so to say, before our very eyes, while the fires of injustice are rank in our nostrils. Our speaker, he went on, is a formidable scholar of this shameful period in the history of France. Listen carefully, because it contains lessons for us at this very moment, here in our noble Temple Academy. It is a tale of lie and libel and deceit, and there is much to glean from it even for such a privileged society as ours. The visitor, it turned out, was too short for the height of the lectern; it rose to the bottom of his chin, so that his head seemed to hover on its own, bodiless. Captain Dreyfus, he said, is an officer in the French military who in a public ceremony of deliberate humiliation has been wrongfully stripped of his epaulets, but here he was interrupted: what are epaulets, sir, are they something like underpants? Against barbs such as this the little man struggled on in what soon became an assault of chatter and titter, as by twosomes and threesomes his audience dwindled. And when I furtively gestured to Ben-Zion Elefantin to come away, he glared at me with a ferocity I did not recognize, and remained where he was.

For days afterward the rowdies made much of this event in their harryings, with taunts of you are rank in my nostril and other such inspired vituperations, stripped epaulets not least among them. And in chapel on Sunday Reverend Greenhill announced that he intended to take a week's holiday in the Hebrides, to follow, he said, in the footsteps of Boswell and Dr. Johnson.

*

September 28, 1949. The exodus is under way. Two have already departed, one to Florida (the hammer-and-tongs fellow, and good riddance), the other ostensibly to vacation in Switzerland, where his nephew has business connections as well as a pied-à-terre in Zurich. I take vacation to be a euphemism for the final adieu: this chap, a veteran of kidney stones, can barely pump out three words without losing his breath, and who knows how he will survive a plane trip of many hours? Next week, I hear, two more of our sorry cohort are to vanish, the first to what is nowadays known as a senior residence, the second to a furnished annex, formerly a garage, directly behind his sister-in-law's home in nearby Bronxville. (His brother is deceased.) As I earlier remarked, the Trustees are far, far from being pinched for dollars, and were never likely to be dependents, yet what else is longevity if not dependency?

We were seven, and then six, and then five, and now with the exit of four, there remains but one, and I am that one. Not that I am entirely alone. Amelia, seeing the imminent collapse of her engagement here, has gone off to Texas with her newest casanova (so says Hedda), but Hedda herself persists. I go down to the kitchen for meals; it simplifies, or else call it democratization. We sit side by side and sometimes together pull out from their shelves in the pantry two or three of Reverend Greenhill's disorderly mélange of old books, unwanted everywhere, though Hedda thinks this inconceivable. Why not take whatever you please, I tell her, they will anyhow end in the dumpster along with the much abused chapel pews. Danke, aber nein, only this one I take, and showed me the title, Liederkreis von Heinrich Heine.

★

September 30, 1949. I had determined to carry what I knew to be my father's foremost treasure to Ben-Zion Elefantin's room, relying on his obstinately shut door to ensure our privacy. But I hung back: it was there, amid the floating dust particles, that we had lain leg over leg, as if trapped together in the soft maze of some spider's web, and under

the shawl of a solitude and gravity that frightened me. My
instinct was to keep away, and my own room, exposed to
any passerby (I was too cowardly to flout the rules), was
anyhow unsuitable for my devising. My devising was, as I
dimly felt it, a consecration of sorts. The chapel was bare
of such sensations, and besides, we had once been discovered there. Then what of Reverend Greenhill's sanctum?
No one entered unless summoned, not even the masters,
though according to his own dictum, Reverend Greenhill's study door was never closed, either by his wish or
by any key. Gentlemen, he once told us (his text that day
was the serpent in Eden), I own nothing of value but my
library and my reflections; my books are mere matter, my
reflections are not. It was off-putting to think (no doubt a
derisive invention of the rowdies) that he kept on his table
a photograph of his dead wife, or was it his dead child,
with a wilting lily before it. But no pupil who was called
to stand at that table had ever reported seeing anything
like this. It was the carpet that surprised, a meadowlike
flourish of purple flowers and curled fronds; it appeared
to be Reverend Greenhill's sole indulgence. We who remembered Mr. Canterbury's introduction of this luxury knew better. And anyhow Reverend Greenhill had
requested before his departure that every middle- and
upper-form boy study his Geography of Great Britain and
put a green mark, if he could find them, on the Hebrides.

As for the carpet: I have since come to believe that monastic zeal conceals a sybarite.

*

October 4, 1949. It was on this carpet that we settled in our customary chess posture, I uneasily on one side, he on the other, with my shoebox between us. I had fixed the hour at eleven that night, when both masters and boys were safely asleep, while in some distant valley Reverend Greenhill, as I supposed, was stalking the spoor of those venerated names I had already forgotten. I am sorry, Ben-Zion Elefantin said, that I declined to come away when you asked. That stupid lecture, what a bore, I said, why would you want to stay? Oh, he said, this man they shamed, he is loyal and they say he is disloyal, it is as if he is Elefantin, but you are my friend and once more I have disappointed you. You haven't, it's just the way you are, I said, and got up to pull aside the curtains at the big paneled windows to let in the light. It was no more than pale misty moonlight, but it was enough; it wouldn't do to switch on the lamp on Reverend Greenhill's table. Even as late as it was, some lone boy on his way to the toilet might see the brightness under the doorsill and spy on us. Look, I said, I've brought you something important. It's only for you, no one else would understand.

And again I told him that my father had once trav-
eled to Egypt, and while sailing upstream on the Nile had
observed on his left the jumbled greenery of Elephantine Island and the white masses of storks crowding the
banks. I told him more: I said that my father, fresh from
Sir Flinders Petrie's tutelage, had recognized from afar
the broken earth mounds of abandoned excavations, and
had ordered his guide to take him ashore. No, the guide
said, there has come recently a very strong khamsin, it
tears up the ground and overturns the ruins, it is not safe
now to tread there. But my father insisted, and the two of
them picked their way through silted stones and newborn
chasms while the guide went on groaning his refusal. It
was here, pulled up from a deep ditch resembling a tunnel,
that my father found what I keep in this box.

The reader may well wonder at these prevarications.
Nothing of the sort is recorded in my father's fading notes
as I have described them here. Under the woolen socks
that covered my shoebox I had hidden what I felt to be
a tribute, a token, a proof, though of what? For a long
time I was unknowing; but now nothing was obscured
and I knew and I knew and I knew. Our knees, our shoulders, our breathings, had touched. It was as if the crisis
of my father's desires were destined to fall upon such a
bony specter as Ben-Zion Elefantin; yet I was in fear of
his repugnance, and of my own diffidence before it. I had
seen how the meek bent of his scrawny shoulders could

flame into an obdurate certainty: would he scoff at my father's chief finding as he had scoffed at all the others? And how could he dare to scoff if I convinced him, however falsely, of my father's credibility? And of the khamsin and the silted stones and the storks?

Then I took out from my shoebox the beaker with its long stork's neck and its one emerald eye.

Here it is, I said, it's for you, I want you to have it. You can show it to your parents to decide if it's real. It can't be fake, my father didn't get it from some shady shopkeeper or anything fishy like that. Look, it's in the shape of a stork! No, he said, not a stork, the body of the ibis is white like a stork's but the beak is black and curved downward. All right, I said, but it's yours anyway, it was meant for you, some day you will be going from here, your parents will send for you. Oh, he said, I can never predict when my uncle will come, and my parents are far away.

I felt his reluctance. I saw that he preferred silence, turning his hungry face to the silhouetted shelves of Reverend Greenhill's books, as if by his look he could swallow them all. The carpet under the deluding moonlight seemed all at once botanically alive, a real garden, with rose-red petals and grass-green stalks, and the beaker standing on its base of avian knees like some wild wayward bird that had lost its way and landed there. The minutes of quiet took on the gravity of the ceremonial, though I could not have named it that, nor am I confident even now of that sacerdotal term. What I knew was only that something crucial, some merciless thirst, was at stake: that my connection, however fearful or tenuous, with Ben-Zion Elefantin must not be cut off. Sooner or later he would leave. Sooner or later I would never see him again. He put out his hand to me and I took it. Thank you, he said, but it is impossible, what is such a vessel to me?

He left me behind then, as one would abandon a person infected by plague. I somehow understood, for a reason I cannot unravel, that this was not the first time he had come to this place in the night.

★

October 7, 1949. My evenings with Hedda in the kitchen are quite pleasant. Only yesterday she confided that she has begun to look for employment elsewhere, but is willing to stay on until I know where I am to go. To my relief, she has agreed to substitute lighter fare for those dense stews, and my digestion is much the better for it. In addition, we have fallen into a practice entirely alien to my experience. I was at first acutely embarrassed. Her idea struck me as a foolish game, and under normal circumstances I believe it would surely be so. She had removed from the pantry shelves (at my urging, it may be recalled) the work of some foreign poet, and not long ago showed me, on facing pages, an English version. She would read aloud from the German, she proposed, and I was to do the same for the translation. I dislike the sounds of that distasteful language, but when I see how at home she is in those growly syllables, and how they transform her from an inconsequential domestic to a woman who thinks, I am, I admit, carried away. I can still remember verbatim all four lines of the verse that uncannily fell to me:

> *At first I almost despaired,*
> *And thought I would never be able to bear it;*
> *Yet even so, I have borne it—*
> *But do not ask me how.*

My lost and dearest Peg, Valorous and Pure. It is as if this long-dead Jew (so Hedda tells me he is), of whom I know nothing, mourns in my own voice.

And here, in the helter-skelter of Reverend Greenhill's books, many with their leaves gnarled by the steam of kettles and stewpots over the years, you have only to put in your hand and pull out a plum: my son's current idée fixe, so to say, unless he has already fled off to other fantasies. I and Thou, a little thing, no thicker than a pamphlet, by this Buber he spoke of. Yet another Jew. I have looked into it: impenetrable.

Hedda's anxious perusal of the help-wanted columns puts me in mind of a public resource I have never before contemplated using. My immediate intention is to place brief advertisements in various newspapers, not excluding the tabloids, in the hope of relieving me of the dread that too often worries my nights. If this small scheme should reveal nothing, well and good. And if a reply should come, what am I to think?

*

October 12, 1949. This morning an extraordinary telephone call from Ned Greenhill. I regret being out of touch, he said, how long has it been since that fine afternoon at the Oyster Bar? I hear they are tearing the place apart and redoing it from scratch, dozens of new hires and so forth, it seems the world doesn't stand still. And how are you in general, Lloyd? Comfortably suspended in lassitude, I told him; but I dislike these obligatory maunderings that conceal an as yet unspoken purpose. Oh yes, he said, everything up in the air, what's to become of the old mausoleum in the woods? That thicket of antediluvian maples always gave me a feeling, especially at night, of wolves prowling there, it wouldn't be a loss to have them come down, roots and all. The real estate section in last week's Tribune, if you happened to see it, was full of probable buyers. Yes, I said, I saw that, and isn't your son one of them? Well Lloyd, he said, it's problematic, the place has a history, not altogether unsavory, and typical of its era after all, so there's some vestige of nostalgia, don't you think, at least for the likes of us elderly fellows. I've told Edwin, keep it low, don't go too high, but this new generation's got no use for such ideas, it's nothing but taller and taller, so how would you feel, Lloyd, about relocating to the fifteenth floor over on East Seventy-sixth? Used to be the old Winthrop Court, Edwin's converting it into a live-in hotel, all the amenities, maid service and so on. And an actual courtyard, a little private garden of shrubs and paths, all hidden from any casual pedestrian eye. Very fine restaurants in the vicinity, as I can personally testify. I know you've all had to get out of that moth-eaten wreck, I heard this only last week from John Theory, turns out he's a classmate of Edwin's at Amherst. It would do you good to get away from the grasshoppers and back into the life of the city, so what do you say? And understand me, Lloyd, except for taxes and suchlike this would be something I hope you'd accept as a tribute from me.

Our conversation went on for more than two hours. He explained that his son planned for the initial tenants to be of a certain standing, in order to lure others of similar status. A prestige building, they call it. And because of our old connection, Ned said, for you, Lloyd, and solely for you, the fifteenth-floor suite has been set aside, if you would accept it, as a lifetime gift from me, though who knows which of us will go graveward first. So Lloyd, he said, you'll think about it, won't you?

Of course I pressed him to tell what could possibly

have motivated this inconceivable gesture. His response was at bottom offensive, and on three counts. First, I am a man of dignified wealth in my own right, not to be regarded as a recipient of another man's benefaction. Second, wittingly or not, he flaunts his son's prosperity when he is fully aware of my own paternal disappointment. Third, lurking below this seeming generosity of heart, is its price: I am to serve as a decoy to further his son's ambition. I had thought better of Ned, but much like his portion of the bulk of mankind, he puts his own interest first, undeniably sugar-coated by reminiscence.

Of his recollections, and his claims, I recognize very little. I knew him from a distance; I knew him hardly at all. In those hurtful years at the Academy, he told me, there were only two persons who regarded him with decency. One was Reverend Greenhill and the other was Lloyd Petrie. You never put me down, Lloyd, you never called me Hebe, and that time when a mob of them came and tore whole pages out of my Greek grammar, you had nothing to do with it. You were among the very few who kept away. I was suffering all those years at school, Lloyd, and it's not something a person forgets. You never went out of your way to do me harm.

I was embarrassed by all this untempered emotion. That is how these people are, their overflowing sentimentalism. Their motion picture style of exaggerated feeling. Well, I said, I do remember that awful night, they had cigarettes and burned holes in your sheets. But why, I asked, did you think I would do any of that sort of thing? Because, he said, you were a Petrie. You were one of them, you thought it was your right.

This, I must acknowledge, unsettled me. I was a Petrie then, and I am a Petrie now. It is for this very reason that Ned, through his son, offers me an advantage, is it not? I could not tell him, if he failed to discern it for himself, that I had been deprived of my right, as he put it, because I had been contaminated by Ben-Zion Elefantin. I dared not tell him how fervently I had longed to be reinstated.

Instead, I firmly declined his largesse.

It is true that I never called him Hebe; but I thought it. And sometimes, I admonish myself, I still think it.

*

October 18, 1949. There has not been a single reply to my numerous advertisements, though with some trepidation at how outlandish it was, I went so far as to place one in the Jewish Day, a local journal whose existence I have only just now come upon. I kept my anonymity, of course, and supplied only a postal box number. My language too was sparse and direct: if you, I wrote, were at any time ever associated with a children's home known as the Elijah Foundation, please respond. A far-fetched effort. Boys of twelve seventy years ago would likely today be dead men.

I am happy not to have uncovered Ben-Zion Elefantin by this means, or anyone who knew him. And better yet, it promises that he was never a boy sent over to the Academy by some shabby almshouse that has not survived. Absence itself is a kind of proof.

★

October 20, 1949. It is by now several days since that abrasive talk with Ned Greenhill. On second thought, I believe I will accept his invitation, but on a gentleman's terms and decidedly sans his benevolence. I am a practical man, as I often say, and the hard truth is that I have nowhere else to lay my head.

As for his son: if these forlorn precincts should fall into his hands, how high will he go?

★

November 3, 1949. For the remainder of that school term I saw far too little of Ben-Zion Elefantin. Something poisonous had come between us: a remoteness beyond my understanding. When he gave me his hand that fevered winter night on the flowered carpet, it was hot and moist, as if he had combed it through dew. I had no inkling that I would never again know the slightness of his palm or the frailty of his small knuckles. And once more his door was shut against me, and again I would catch the bleats and driftings of what passed for liturgical grumbles, or else the muted wail of some secret weeping; but he was two years older than I, and thereby too old to cry. I, alone on my bed with my disordered chessboard before me, was not.

In the refectory he sat at a distance, and I saw that he spoke to no one, and no one spoke to him. But at certain unaware moments I would feel his look. It was, I thought, altogether washed clean of the meek and the humble. In chapel too he kept apart, and was intent, as always, on the sermon, though of late Reverend Greenhill's homiletics had departed from the biblical, and for several Sundays in a row he chose as his theme his recent adventures in the Hebrides. His holiday there, he said, had been inspired by Samuel Johnson, a famous Englishman of virtue and wisdom who lived two hundred years ago; and also by James Boswell, a Scotsman equally famous and virtuous. The loyalty to each other of these two friends, he told us, was such that Boswell gave his life to recording the life of Johnson, particularly during a journey to the Hebrides the two of them together undertook.

It was clear that he meant us to seize the meaning of this lesson: friendship and loyalty and attentiveness and decorum. (To illustrate the latter, he read out a paragraph of Boswell's prose.) All this, I saw, was aimed at the row-dies; but they kept their heads down and were quiet. Or else were drawn in by his tale of crags and abysses, and of ships broken on rocks in the waters that skirt the islands, and especially of a frightening fall from a mossy cliff. (Here, in a sort of purposeful drama, Reverend Greenhill held up his elbow, fractured and healing, he said, but painful still.) And I thought: I have been loyal to Ben-Zion Elefantin, how unfair that he is disloyal to me.

Today as I write (in one of these formless fits of longing and loss that sometimes flood me), it occurs to me to ask: in the many pages of my memoir that heap up under my hand, am I not Ben-Zion Elefantin's Boswell? It discomfits me to think that if I am Boswell, the small figure I was once so achingly devoted to imagined himself to be Dreyfus.

*

November 12, 1949. I have spoken before of those wretched showers of our youth: a common space of two overhead nozzles, heated by a coal stove that spat out its fickle warmth no more than inches from its maw. Two showerheads to serve one hundred pupils, with five minutes allotted for each, no matter the season; but from November to March the queue was not long. A boy would prefer to stink, and many did, rather than endure the frigid air of this glacial hell, or the water that was colder than air. It was here that I found myself unexpectedly alone with Ben-Zion Elefantin. He stood before me wet and naked

and shivering, and I the same before him; but the blaze of
his hair was darkened by water, and his ribs were as skeletal as his pitiful knees. His bare feet were paler than his
hands. Without his cap and his blazer, he seemed smaller
than ever. Nearly a month had gone by with not a syllable
between us. I felt a little afraid; what must I say?

I asked him why.

He said nothing. So again I asked why.

Because I believed you were my friend.

I *am* your friend, I said.

And again he said nothing. You have to tell me why, I
said, you have to.

A cloud of vapor spilled out of his mouth, and I saw
the same rise up from mine. It was hard to breathe in that
place.

But it's real. You saw for yourself that it's real. And
your parents, you told me they buy and sell such things.

They keep me safe from them. That is why I am sent
to school. To keep me from abomination.

I knew this word. Mr. Canterbury had spoken it in
chapel many times.

And it was Ben-Zion Elefantin's last word to me. I can
hear it now, in a kind of self-willed hallucination: that
curiously wavering uncharted bookish voice of his own
making. An orphaned voice of no known origin.

★

December 12, 1949. No uncle came for him. He remained with the Fourth Form, moved up to the Fifth and the Sixth and the Seventh, and I, in the Eighth, later that year, in June, wore cap and gown for Commencement. The ceremony was held in a capacious tent on the football field, equipped with row upon row of folding chairs to accommodate the mass of parents and well-wishers who were expected to attend. Or were, perhaps, not entirely expected, which may have explained why Reverend Greenhill had appointed the Seventh Form to fill most of the empty places, should there be any. At one side was the dais on which the graduates were to congregate, and at the other a long table freighted with lemonade and cinnamon ices and strawberries and scones heavily blanketed by chocolate syrup and caramel cream, the last an innovation of Reverend Greenhill's. (I heard him remark to one of the visitors that this violation of a traditional Scottish biscuit might not appeal to a fastidious palate, but the graduates were, after all, still boys.) As the procession shuffled forward to the blare of some hidden operatic loudspeaker, one could see a scattering of fathers, and with them the young women who from their age and attire, I now speculate, might be second wives, or even former nannies. The mothers, with their uplifted faces, were seated nearer the lectern, where Reverend Greenhill waited for the sounds of Aida to ebb. (My own mother was not among them. She had sent me a congratulatory note, fearing she would be too fatigued to sustain the long festivities.) First came the lesser prizes: for Attentiveness, for Patience, for Enterprise, for Courtesy, for Equestrian Skills, and all the rest; and then the Award for Excellence in Latin, renamed Classics (to include private study of Greek), won, predictably, by Edwin J. Greenhill. And following this, the Headmaster's Oration. Gentlemen, Reverend Greenhill began, I mean not to orate, but rather to bless. As you embark on this new phase of your lives, I hope you will carry with you the aspirations and virtues of our time-honored Academy, and that each of you will strive, as you grow into men, to be both a scholar and yes, a gentleman. But a scholar can be cruel, and a gentleman can be coarse. And here he read out, in his thin but reassuring voice, two passages from Scripture, the first from the Old Testament, the second from the New, in that order, he said, especially to note how the New and the Old are in harmony. A Jew named Abraham, he said, hastened to succor three parched strangers, and gave them water, and fed them, and cooled them from the sun in the shade of a tree, all unaware that they were angels. In the same way, we learn in the Gospel of Luke how a Samaritan, neither Jew nor Christian, found on the highway a man who had been beaten and robbed and lay nearly dead, and carried him to an inn and cared for him like a brother. And so, though I wish each graduate of our beloved Temple Academy for Boys to excel as a scholar and a gentleman, I hope that you will, above all, be kind.

Familiarity brought tedium. I half-heard all this, and at so distant a time I can barely give its gist. Besides, so commonplace in chapel were these exhortations, they might well have been tattooed on the palms of our hands. As for me, I had my eye on a brilliant red blemish at the edge of that restless puddle of Seventh Formers who had come to swell the assembly. Ben-Zion Elefantin was now fifteen, and nearly as small as before. I tried to catch his look, but his watchfulness seemed inward: on this day of farewell was he thinking of me, of how he cast me away for some preternatural cause? Was my father's stork, with its blinded eye, the abomination, or was it I?

Really, I ask myself to this very hour, was it I?

★

January 26, 1950. A catastrophe. How could this have happened? I blame it on my increasing forgetfulness, but how could I have forgotten what clings fast to my heart? Or perhaps I did not forget it, and those burly defectors Hedda called back from the city to pack up my things (one hundred or so boxes) carelessly left it behind? Too late now to retrieve it. Worse yet, given its weakened carriage and its increasing rust (that vinegar bath), was it mistaken for debris, and disposed of? The wrecking ball, I hear, has already had its way. So here I sit, with a bottle of ink before me, and my old Montblanc grudgingly resurrected (I had to replace the nib). In my eyrie on the highest floor of this solid old building the new windows admit no street noises, and the walls are inches thick. In this place no one could complain of my Remington! And I have nothing else as a sign of what was. Her grave is far away.

I am no longer accustomed to longhand, it tires my palsied wrists. (With my Remington it was the shoulders.) And even so fine a pen as a Montblanc can sometimes falter on a thin sheet of paper and spurt a droplet of ink; the cuff of my sleeve is spattered. No matter. I can see ahead almost to the close of my memoir; I am loath to put paid to it now. (I despise unfinished effort, as I have often reminded my son.) And then what will become of it? What of value or interest can it have? I have all along spoken of my reader, but can such a chimera exist? These days I sometimes feel as if I myself am a chimera: I walk the city streets in a cloud of uncertainty. I hardly know which way to turn, which is East and which is West. What was once second nature (the life of offices all around me, the lunches, the drinks, the handshake) dizzies me a little, the sidewalk density, the careless mob of unseeing people one must sidestep to avoid collision. Here and there the dirty pigeons, and overhead no birds. The absence of birds! The sky turned zigzag by the contours of this and that high-rise. And no trees.

It was my good fortune to have the December 15th date of eviction put off, though it inconvenienced the scheduled demolition and the difference affected the cost (which I was satisfied to reimburse). Ned Greenhill, or was it his son, managed to persuade Morgan (via John Theory) to allow me to remain through the holidays. Strange as it was, I spent Christmas Eve with Hedda in the kitchen. When Temple House was new, and the Trustees numbered twenty-five and the staff thirty-two, how convivial we were, all those fine fellows now long gone, the gossip, the overblown stories of old business triumphs, the somewhat modest tree (artificial, but genuine silver and costly), the feasting (stuffed goose and liver terrine and buttered shallots and curried lamb), and up and down the table, an infinite row of wines. And while I speak of remembered holidays, I am unhappy to mention that childhood's Christmases were more somber. The fir with its fragile colored glass globes and its gilt star nearly touching the ceiling, and the gaudily wrapped presents below, among them, I knew, the standard toy army and, one glorious year, my coveted chessmen. (Wooden, but I had dreamed of ivory.) And sometimes, when my mother seemed out of sorts and complained of feeling sick, it was only the two of us: my saddened father and I.

In our doomed and abandoned Temple House, Hedda had enlivened the kitchen as well as she could, hanging red and green crepe-paper streamers from cabinet door to cabinet door. The dinner, she told me, was to be anything I desired, but dessert must be a Viennese treat. I dreaded another Sacher torte; too much sugar makes my teeth ache. The pots on the stove were steaming as always, and while the oven was baking whatever it might be, I was not unpleased to go on with our whimsical game. Hedda surprised me instead with what I supposed was a Christmas song (she had learned it in kindergarten, she said, and still remembered every word), as well as a scrap of paper in her own striving half-English. To me it has no holiday resonance of any kind, but I put it in my pocket and keep it still, if only to take note of Hedda's Teutonic script; and I record it here, I hardly know why.

A pine tree high in the North he lonely stands.
Under snow and wind he sleeps.
A palm tree he dreams a land to the East,
traurig on the desert sand.

If these words can claim some coherent sense, I cannot discern it; but when Hedda sang them in her emotional

German, she appeared to feel its meaning. Her eyes were wet. North, East, what fleeings, what unwilled supplantings? The author, she reminded me, is the very one who echoed the loss of my darling Peg.

Yet the Christmases referenced above are, if I may say so, boilerplate. Certainly I favor tradition; I am aware that ancestral decorum ought not to be scorned. The aberrant is to be shunned. Life's fundamental rhythms depend on sameness, not deviation. All this I long ago learned from my mother.

Hedda's dessert turned out to be an elaborate pancake called (a name I cannot pronounce) Kaiserschmarren, filled with caramelized almonds and raisins soaked in rum. It did make my teeth ache; but the rum, she said, would numb the pain, and she brought out a sizable bottle and a cup for each of us, and poured a second cup, and a third, and at last a fourth, and then it was midnight. Enough there is yet also for New Year's, Hedda said, nicht wahr?

An anomaly. Out of the ordinary. A deviation from the natural. This homeless old man, this wandering Jewess.

★

January 27, 1950. These furnishings, these tables and chairs and credenzas and whatnot, make me uneasy. I suppose such modern geometries are the fashion in hotels that pretend to the comforts of luxury. Rectangular surfaces, ruler-straight legs, steel tops, nothing cushioned, nothing rounded. The bed, with its excessive pillows (they strain my back), has the width, or so it seems, of a horizonless continent. In the night, under a far-off ceiling, I see no end of vacuity. I feel myself a stranger in this bed, as I have not felt since my Academy cell: that narrow hard bed, my shoebox hidden beneath and my chessboard teetering on a bumpy blanket above. (And Ben-Zion Elefantin silently pondering.) Or not since the bed in which my son was conceived.

My Peg's sweet bed, there I was never a stranger.

*

January 29, 1950. Hedda telephones now and then (she is still unemployed), asking how I am, are my new surroundings pleasant, and so on; but as her world is scarcely akin to mine, I trust these exchanges will soon fade away.

*

February 2, 1950. The disadvantage of such a high floor is the beating of the wind on the panes. A disturbing noise, different from the tapping of rain. (There are times when the latter mimics the persistent diligence of my old Remington.) But a wild winter wind, especially at night, is frightening, like some misunderstood warning.

★

February 4, 1950. The reader, if he has not already abandoned me, will be reminded that he has been deliberately
banned from viewing the contents of my father's cigar
box. During the confusion and may I say the distress of
my relocation, I myself rarely looked into it, but even
now, while I have the leisure to parse its perplexities (and
a lone nightly meal in a reputed restaurant turns out to be
less appealing than the kitchen in Temple House), I am
unable to fathom its origin or its mode. For want of something more plausible, I have on occasion described these
papers as a transcription. And again as a plea. And again as
a deposition. But for all their particularity, there is nothing verbatim here, and how could there be? I remember
nothing. I remember everything. I believe everything. I
believe nothing. The frenzied murmurings of two agitated
boys prone and under a spell. A liar's screed, an invention?
An apparition's fevered pedantry? And who knows such
things, this garble of history and foreign babble? Not I.
Nor am I a man of imagination.

Still, I must decide. Destroy what cannot be accounted
for, or dispatch it all, and the cigar box itself, to the vault
where the Academy History lies open to access by scholars.
Already, I hear, the History is not infrequently consulted
by persons with an interest in nineteenth- and early-
twentieth-century Anglicized education. (If my reader is

such a one, he should recall that for the use of citations he ought of course to ask permission of Morgan.)

I shrink from the latter course more out of caution than fear. To honor my father's memory, I am obliged to defend the family name. I foresee that to submit for preservation an eccentricity so extreme may easily provoke accusations of innate instability, not to say lunacy. At my father's graveside, I recall, my poor mother, ringed round by Wilkinsons, was made to endure the mutterings of such calumnies: hence the probability of disgrace.

It is betrayal that terrifies. Often and often in my cowardly memoir, I have been tempted to claim Ben-Zion Elefantin's voice. Logic insists on it. Reason demands it. Logic and reason are themselves cowardly. What is it I am afraid to consent to? That I am beguiled by the enigma of memory? And can memory, like dream, fabricate what ordinary consciousness cannot?

*

February 7, 1950. Of late I have been reconsidering the usefulness of having my father's artifacts appraised. What point to my keeping them here in this modernist den, where newness is king? Who will care for them as my father cared, and I after him? Who will be moved by their antiquity? For my son, who never knew his grandfather and anyhow shuns the ancestral, an inheritance of this kind can be no more than an unwanted burden. (As when the Irish maid, with her repellent brogue, recoils from what she calls my filthy pots and ugly dolls.)

Nevertheless, it may be that my father in his Egyptian ramblings may have happened upon objects of actual consequence, worthy perhaps of some museum vitrine. My hope is that a curator's expertise may validate (dare I say it?) his life. My own craving I keep underground: only suppose that this red-kneed beaker should in fact prove to be the last remnant of Khnum on that stork-mobbed island in the middle of the Nile?

And if so?

*

February 9, 1950. The decision is made. So certain am I of its rectitude that I would engrave it in stone if I could. I will dispose of my memoir. Possibly I will quietly place it in the trash for the maid to remove. Possibly I will find a more trustworthy solution: but I will be rid of it.

A consultant from the Metropolitan Museum's History of Near Eastern Art department has agreed to view my father's artifacts. He makes no promises. So many of these amateur collections, he told me, reflect the collector's enthusiasm more than his skills or his judgment. That your father worked for a season with Sir Flinders

Petrie and engaged with him privately is delightful to know, but entirely irrelevant. And that he retained notes from those conversations, even if of papyri and temples, may be of some personal interest to his son, but is hardly more generally useful. More frequently than not, what is brought to our attention is meaningless detritus, or worse, inept forgeries.

It disappointed me that despite my insistence on the authenticity of Sir Flinders Petrie's signature, he declined so much as to glance at my father's notebook. His dismissal persuades me also to destroy it. If for the expert it holds no scientific or historical value, it must carry the same peril as my memoir. And should after my demise those oddments of my Wilkinson cousins (they are included in my will) come upon either notebook or memoir, their ill-natured suspicions of my father's madness will be confirmed.

My father, then, was an enthusiast. That he anointed his Cousin William, that he was besotted with Cousin William for all of his days, was that mad?

*

February 12, 1950. Lincoln's Birthday. The question of the deposition, as I hereafter will term it, secreted in this faintly odorous antiquated box: I must finally call it a deposition, as if it were somehow rendered under oath, never mind that its authorship is ambiguous. Or if it is instead an apologia pro vita sua, then whose entrails is it exposing, whose disordered will?

I am today taken by surprise by a parcel sent to me here from Morgan Bank. John Theory writes that though the late Reverend Henry McLeod Greenhill's library had suffered constant serious deterioration due to the unfortunate location of its place of storage, in addition to the ravages of insect infestation, and could not be preserved, it seemed prudent to draw up an inventory of its holdings as a supplement to the History of the Temple Academy for Boys by Many Hands (1915), kept here in the vault containing other pertinent Academy materials for which Morgan is now responsible, including an unattributed Sargent portrait of the author Henry James, Jr. And since you, his letter continues, as the sole remaining Trustee whose present address is known, and in view of your ongoing interest in the Academy, a copy of said inventory is herewith enclosed. With kind regards, JT.

These multitudinous lists consist of scores and scores of esoteric titles, some in German and French, a cluster of Greek and Latin grammars, a threadbare copy of Gibbon's Decline and Fall of the Roman Empire, whole shelves of theological studies (Augustine, Origen, Tertullian, and so forth), a History of the Jews (translated from the German, with pencilled notes), and an abundance of volumes related to the early Levant: Development of Epigraphy;

Tells of Mesopotamia, Babylon, Nimrud, and Nineveh; Yahweh and the Gods of Canaan, and on and on.

One title among the last catapults me, if I may put it so, into wild surmise. I give it below, as it appears in the inventory:

The Israelite Temple on Elephantine Island, Volume II. Reconstructive diagrams. Maps, including surrounding area. History of tripartite temples. The Khnumian cultic niche. Author: Douglas C. Hesse, Ph.D. Oriental Press, 1912. [Volume I missing.]

Volume I missing? How? Where? Into whose fancies did it go? And what is it that unnerves me so?

*

February 17, 1950. The building is being rapidly populated. When I go down for my walk, I am no longer alone in the elevator. Three or four times a week a young Japanese woman and her little son join me there. Her face is flawless porcelain, and I think of Miranda's favorite vase (the willowy maiden on the bridge) and its pride of place on that mahogany console I so much disliked. In our companionable two-minute descent I learn that her husband is second in rank at the Japanese consulate. At half-past three, when school is out, the lobby, with its hideous spider-legged Saarinen chairs (so I am told they are called), is clamorous with the squeals of a flock of children, nearly all of them accompanied by white-shoed nannies. I have yet to see here the silver heads of widows and widowers: am I the only aged occupant? My own silver head is thoroughly overlooked, my name unrecognized: all these ripe and pulsing lives making their way, climbing their rungs, bedding their beloveds, have no use for a retired Trustee of a forgotten patrician academy.

I am no one's decoy. I live here on the strength of another boy's honest gratitude. And for what? That a Petrie never called him Hebe?

*

February 18, 1950. When I am at times too fatigued for my afternoon walk, I sit in the lobby on these comfortless chairs to watch the children come home from school. They put me in mind of birds, always flitting, always chirping, and their quick eyes dart like the eyes of birds, and their cheeks are round and their little brown shoes are buckled and their satchels are of many colors, and when they shout, as they often do, they make a tangled soprano chorus. Strange to find myself among children after years of mouldering in the company of old men. I have picked out one or two of my favorites, the small Japanese boy, always with his mother, and an older girl whose unaware breasts, as I imagine, are already budding. Now and then I catch sight of a child of perhaps eleven or twelve who seems to hold himself apart, and never romps as the others do, but hurries away, though I never see where, and before I can steal a glance at his face. What marks him for me is his blood-red hair.

*

March 12, 1950. For the last few weeks I have not been entirely myself, and while the weather is bright and I am exacting in my dress even when confined, I am never tempted to walk. I am content enough with the services offered here, despite the incompetence of the laundress who delivers my personal things: time after time, this annoyance of mismatched socks carelessly returned to their drawer where I habitually find them. Luckily, among the promised amenities is a personal shopper who replenishes my socks (without getting rid of the useless singles), and also my shirts, continually speckled with ink on the sleeves. Nor do I miss sitting alone at a restaurant table, while the tables all around are noisy with prattle and cackle. As for room service, the trays arrive on a prettified cart, and depart with not a word beyond Sir and Good

Morning. Even the wretched Amelia, and surely Hedda with her Freud and her stews and her Heine, gave proof of the reality of human flesh.

So I turn again and again to the riddles in my father's cigar box. Not to pass the time, as old people do, but out of an insistence that grapples me more and more. I am hypnotized, if you will, by a certain passage in the deposition: the capsule of all. The significant thing, the significant thing. It shakes me, it unmans me. I mean to penetrate the intent of those implausible traders in search of an implausible goal. (And wasn't my father just such a trader?) Is it, the significant thing, made of clay, of stone, what form does it take, is it weighty, is it slight, is it palpable at all, like a body or a bird? Or is it a fanatical dream? Then whose?

Or is it a mighty idea?

★

May 30, 1950. Memorial Day. Since henceforth I will have no reader, I need not say by what means I have disposed of my memoir, and my father's notebook with it. Enough to know that they are, like all things treasonous, banished.

The deposition itself I have concealed where only my son is likely to find it when he comes to search among my personal effects to choose how I am to be clothed for my burial. (There will be no funeral.) Hence I can freely disclose in these final reflections the site of its unearthing: a cigar box beneath the innumerable socks accumulated in a crowded drawer.

I have not been well for many weeks. The doctor who serves this place belittles my complaints. Not illness, he asserts. Social malaise, that despicable cant. No letters come, and except for the obituaries (so many of my peers, familiar names) I have lost all concern for the newspaper's cataclysms.

I have had a single visitor. Hedda, uninvited. Surprisingly, on the advice of the defectors that there were still jobs to be had, she is now employed as one of the newer cooks at the Oyster Bar. She was eager to tell that she had lately observed a Judge Greenhill at a table with a view of the ramp, a lebhaftig and talkative old man, and can it be true that I knew him as a child at the Academy? (I did see that Ned's wife died early in April.) She brought me a pastry, charmingly wrapped. I am afraid our conversation was sparse. She wished me well and departed.

But I cannot eat something so unbearably sweet.

*

I give this writing no date. I am unsure of the date. I dislike putting on my shoes. The windows cannot be opened. There are no fans here in summer. The air conditioning blows cold.

I think I know the significant thing. Ben-Zion Elefantin too knows the significant thing.

Only the two of us know.

Not in the heavens, not in the sea, not a god made of stone buried in the earth. A temple in a lost kingdom of storks on the Nile, is that what it is?

Only the two of us know.

We two kings.

The Bloodline of the Alkanas

Cyrus Alkana was my father, and if you can recognize this name, you belong to an inconspicuous substratum of humanity—a coterie, if such things can still be said to exist. He had his little following, cranks and fanatics like himself, including an out-of-favor critic who once dubbed him "the American Keats." If this was launched as a compliment, it landed as a disparagement. Keats was exactly the trouble, the reason for my father's obscurity—and not only Keats, but Shelley and Wordsworth and Coleridge and Tennyson and Swinburne, all those denizens of a fading antiquity. It wasn't that my father worshiped these old poets who had crowded the back pages of his grade-school spelling book—he regarded himself as one of their company, a colleague and companion.

It was presumed by his enemies (he had many more

of these than readers) that his formal literary education had stopped with those spellers—at sixteen he left Thrace High School in upstate New York for a job as a copyboy at the *Beacon-Herald*, the local newspaper, snatching stories fresh from the typewriter to speed them to the big clattering linotype machines. He wasn't so much running away from school as he was running away from home— there was something at home he didn't like, some influence or threat that repelled him. It couldn't have been his parents, because my father always behaved like a man who had been lavishly nurtured, and in marrying my mother he had lucked into the same cushioned indulgence. Still, some element of family there was that he wanted never again to be close to—a raving sister in an attic, or a herd of brutish cousins who habitually beat him up? He never hinted at anything of the kind; I never heard him speak of family at all. The little that came drifting down to me was only that he lived by himself in a rooming house until he could stiffen his spine for the move to New York. If I had an aunt, even a mad one, I was never to know it.

It was this cramped beginning that led him to the harvesting of enemies. The American Keats, they mocked, was no more than a small-town autodidact. Modernism had left him behind, or else he had never been aware of its arrival, dizzied as he was by groves and rivulets and dawns and goddesses and nymphs. His mind was afloat with cosmic visions—infinity, and transcendence, and the sublime. Which was the least of it: born into the wrong century, he sometimes spattered his lines with *'tis* and *o'er* and *e'en*. These, my mother said in my father's defense, were conscious grace notes, not, as his accusers claimed, outlandish bad habits.

My mother regularly defended my father: it was he alone who was taking a stand for Beauty, lately driven from the world by the conspiracy of a self-styled avant-garde who despised not merely the cradlings of iambic pentameter, but the very skein and pith of magic and mystery.—All this, in fact, was how my mother spoke. She had long ago learned to be a copy of my father. She even copied his distaste for me.

At nine I had begun to dismantle all the clocks in our apartment, and soon discovered how to reassemble their parts. Out of waxed paper, school paste, and bits of wood pried from the backs of picture frames I built frag- ile model airplanes, with the thinnest of wing struts. At twelve, on purpose to provoke, I announced that I had seen God, and that His name was Geometry. (My father dismissed God; he cared only for the gods.) I was absorbed by shapes and their measurements, the height and width of tables and bureaus and doors, everything hard to the touch and substantially *there*. I determined early on that I would shun the vapor of words my parents exhaled, as from some mist-producing internal fungus—my moth- er's, being imitative, somehow more egregious than my father's. These enveloping clouds of words, and the rapture they induced, my father called "the Bestowal." It was a term I heard often, especially in relation to its absence in me.

"The child lacks it," he would say.

"She is wanting in it," my mother would agree.

They had named me Sidney (mistakenly, my father pointed out) after a pair of antiquated poets born centuries apart: Sir Philip Sidney and Sidney Lanier, both of whom, my mother frequently reminded me, "were known to work in your father's vein." She spoke as if they had long ago publicly acknowledged their debt to Cyrus Alkana. I had never cared enough to look up either one.

The Bestowal had come, according to my father, through an ancestral line leading back as far as the poet-prophets Micah and Isaiah, but more immediately through a rumor of one Rafael Alkana, who was said to have set down torrents of God-praises, in rhyming Ladino couplets, in the margins of his prayerbook. In the Inquisitional trauma of that distant fifteenth-century departure from a myth-clad Iberia to an equally shrouded Anatolia, the sacred volume was lost—in shipwreck or conflagration, whichever version one preferred.

"Lost yet not lost," my father said, "whence, even in the latter-day idiom of the New World, the power of language suffuses the bloodline of the Alkanas." And recited:

Frigate or trireme,
Oarsmen or steam,
Onward they ploughed,
Spirits unbowed,
Unto the invincible dream.

Though *whence* and *unto* were recognizably also among his grace notes, it was unclear whether these lines were his own, or a fragment of some admired minor lyrical Victorian.

I did not understand my father's talk. I sensed only that there was some undeniable connection between these enigmatic outbursts and the mundane truth that we were always worrying about money. I was by then a demanding fifteen, shamed by the way we lived in a three-room flat on the fifth floor of a Bronx walkup. The kitchen window looked out on a narrow shaft that plummeted down into a bleak courtyard mobbed by rows of metal barrels. I slept on a pull-out bed abutting a steam radiator, on top of which the current crop of my father's books was heaped, so that in winter I was assaulted by the peculiar odor of heated binding glue.

These books, it was my habit to notice, were never the same for long. They changed their colors and thicknesses—some were squat, some tall and lean, and most had slips of paper, my father's scribbles, stuck between the leaves.

They all came from the public library at the end of our street, a red-brick Carnegie whose coal furnace shook the building with its winter roar. This was as far into the outer world as my father was willing to go. "He lives in his head," my mother insisted, and by this she meant me to grasp that my father's cerebrations were the equivalent of what other fathers had: a regular job. And more: in that labyrinthine space, she implied, were museums and galleries and opera houses and lecture halls and cathedrals and landscapes and monuments: the whole of civilization. If his mind was a kind of Parthenon, then what need had he of the common street?

For herself, though, it was different, and for a certain brief period during my childhood (it didn't long outlast my father's contempt), she ran off to the trolley stop on weekend evenings to begin a rattling journey to the city's buzz and hum. There were free excitements everywhere, in cafés and parks and lofts and barrooms so dark you could scarcely see the faces around you, where readers stood at ill-lit lecterns and shot out ugly staccato syllables, the women in shawls and sandals, the half-bald men dangling mournful gray hanks of hair from behind their ears. Sometimes, to rid my father of what he scorned as my prattle, she took me with her. I disliked these forced excursions and their puffed-up dronings. Once, as a bribe, she bought for me from a street vendor a mechanical toy with many moving parts—by shifting them cleverly, you could construct a tunnel or a tower or a bridge. But mostly she went alone, returning breathless and exhilarated, and smelling foully of cigarette. "Barbarians!" she called out to my father. "Nothing down there but ranting pygmies, rotten as rat's hair, no *music* in it, no *sense*, no *vision*, there's not one in the bunch worth Cyrus Alkana's fingernail clippings—"

Still, whatever supernal faculty the Bestowal may have conferred on my father, it was she who paid the rent.

"He hadn't planned on it, not in the least," she told me when, embarrassed, I went on pressing her: why, unlike other men, was my father content to remain unemployed? "Upstate was a desert for a mind like that, so when he came down to New York he thought he'd find work in a publishing house, even if he hadn't a shred of ordinary credentials—they all wanted a college degree. It didn't impress those fools that he'd read absolutely everything. In fact," she reminded me—it was an anecdote I knew by heart—"when I first set eyes on your father, it was in the cellar of a used-book store on Fourth Avenue, and he had his nose in Pindar, of all things!"

I never troubled to discover who or what this Pindar was; it was enough to know that if not for my mother's enchantment in that damp Fourth Avenue cellar twenty years before, I might have been spared the Alkana bloodline. Instead, three months short of what was to have been her graduation from Vassar, my mother took a job as a receptionist in a small law firm not far from the Bronx Zoo, where she could occasionally hear the barks of the sea lions in their outdoor pool; and then began her life as Cyrus Alkana's shield and support. It was a blessing, she said, that he had been forcibly exempted from the tedious workaday world of offices. Her credo—on behalf of my father—was, she informed me, Solitude and Time, those faithful begetters of the muses. Cyrus Alkana's exaltations were not to be distracted by the shabby incursions of the everyday. Most evenings, when she was too tired or impatient to cook, she would bring us dinner in paper cartons from a local eatery, and would soon sit down to the secondhand Remington that occupied the farther end of the kitchen table, a kind of shrine dedicated to my father's papers, many of them accumulated in overflowing folders. Here she would transcribe Solitude and Time's daily yield, emitting joyful little chirps while tapping away until past midnight.

But my father's exertions were not always the melodious lines of those squarish sonnets and spreading odes that so excited my mother. Often—too often—they were raging letters flung out to his enemies and detractors, and though my mother might plead and remonstrate, she trusted finally in the sacral might of his every outcry, and in the respectful eye of a just posterity. It fell to me to witness the composition of these diatribes, how he splashed them out ferociously with every dip into the ink bottle (my father despised fountain pens), and how he exulted in wickedly ingenious imprecations, oblivious to my watchfulness. Until she came to type them at night, my mother regularly missed these afternoon thunderings— she would depart early in the morning for the sea lions' chorus, while my school day ended at three; I had all the advantage of seeing Cyrus Alkana actually at work. I had been given my own key, with instructions not to disturb my father's labors.

And sometimes there were no labors. I would find my father in my parents' bedroom, lying down, shoeless, with his pale naked feet dangling like animal parts, and his dusty socks curled at one elbow. This pleased me. It meant I would have the kitchen to myself, and could slam the icebox door if I liked, or crackle cookie wrappers without being reprimanded. I was tempted to slip back into the bedroom to stare down at him—it was my only chance to look at my father without having him look back at me. He had a way of twisting his lower lip to show his disappointment. I felt he always saw in me the work of some jealous spirit (he pretended to believe in such things), his bad luck in having spawned an Alkana perversely passed over by the whims of the Bestowal. He had small close-set very black eyes rimmed by short sparse reddish lashes, placed not quite horizontally (the left one seemed to list toward an ear) in a big head made bigger by a bulky bush of red hair. His eyebrows too were red.

Adam, he liked to say, was made of red clay, but his own ruddiness was inherited from King David; I think he was burdened by the inescapable notice it commanded. A tiny tic or tremor went on pulsing through the shut lids. He was sleeping deeply, snoring with drumlike monotony. It was somehow understood between us that I was not to disclose these instances of idleness to my mother. She was confident that his ambition, like her belief in him, was indefatigable.

And it was because of her relentless advocacy that my father began at last to see his things in print. "His things"—this was how my mother, who rarely spoke simply, spoke of Cyrus Alkana's elevated verse. It was the simplicity of humbled gratitude: she knew herself to be the privileged guardian of a fabled cache of royal jewels about to be put out for public display. Each a peerless emerald or pearl, they had all, one by one, been denied publication by this or that obtuse periodical. But my mother had been too shy. Her newest idea was that a volume of these resplendent strophes, strung together like some priceless Oriental necklace, must irresistibly dazzle even the dullest editorial eye—in pursuit of which she typed, she admired, she inspired, she burnished, and you could almost say she influenced. And certainly she wrapped the finished product in carefully smoothed-out brown paper cut from grocery bags, and wrote down the publisher's address in her best Palmer script, and carried the precious package to the post office to be weighed and stamped and sent off to its fate. In our family, it was my mother who was in charge of outgoing mail.

But because one's fate is what one must create (her favorite homily), she had already set in motion something else. On a rainy Saturday afternoon, when my father had gone out, hatless as always, his hair jutting floridly over his ears, on one of his impulsive rambles to the public library, I heard my mother at the Remington, typing more slowly than usual, stopping and then starting again, with long silences in between. It was not her ordinary pace, that rapid and even cadence of a practiced amanuensis.

She looked up when she felt me watching from the doorway.

"Don't dare ask me what I'm doing," she ordered. "I have to *think*—can't you see I'm thinking?"

"About what?"

"Getting them to pay attention. Publishers. Editors. You have to have a hook—"

It wasn't, I knew, that she thought me worthy of being her confidante; but since a conspirator must have an accomplice, even if an inferior one, she earnestly pumped out the rest: "A celebratory imprimatur. An introduction, a kind of preamble. Or call it a preface. That's what I'm doing."

Whatever she was finally willing to name it, it described the poet's circumstances from his birth in backward Thrace to the present flowering of his genius, citing his resemblance to the grandest bards of Albion— and it went off together with each brown-paper packet. Whether or not the tone of these glorifications was persuasive, I could not judge; it was out of my ken and over my head. And my father, it seemed, was kept out of it from the start. Yet what came of it all was three startlingly immediate offers of publication, one from a respected old press (this she quickly dismissed), and the others from two large commercial houses known for their popular successes.

My mother was elated. "We'll go with the biggest fish," she told me. "A reward for swallowing the bait."

The biggest fish, she admitted, had proposed a minnow of an advance while stipulating a single indispensable condition: that the bait be included in the body of the book itself as an enticing illumination of Cyrus Alkana's lines. I saw her hesitate; she had to think it over, she said. She had schemed it only as a worm on a hook, she hadn't expected to go public with it. In the end she had to agree—why lose the big fish for the sake of withholding the inconsequential worm? And the bait, she privately confessed—but only to me, her reluctant confederate— was this: the sole signatory to the gushing endorsement she had quietly fabricated was Alexander Alcott.

It was a name even I could recognize. You couldn't speak, in those years, of an Eliot or a Pound, without, for fairness, adding an Alcott. Alexander Alcott, I knew, was chief among my father's enemies, routinely reviled together with those graven grand luminaries, the acknowledged titans of modernism. That such rarefied figures could be so readily familiar to me, I owed to my father's raucous and tireless hatreds.

"But does he know you've done that?" I asked.

My mother let out an impatiently innocent grunt. "Does who know what?"

"Alexander Alcott. That you used his name that way."

"Oh, I don't need that fool's permission for anything. Besides, I told them over there that I had it—publishers make such fusses over nonsense."

"But what if he finds out and sues?"

"Lawyer talk at your age? Sidney dear, you're a bit of a fool yourself, aren't you? He's bound to find out—think of the publicity that's coming! It won't make a bit of difference to him, he's got fame enough to spare, and he's worthless anyhow. The fellow's nothing but a pestilence, and these days it's pestilence that wins the prizes and the prestige. He's *listened* to, more's the pity, his rubbish gets taught in the schools, he's in all the anthologies, and Lord knows your father isn't, not yet—"

She went on in this way, and though I resented being called a fool, I was more frightened than hurt. I thought her horribly reckless.

A good-sized volume of Cyrus Alkana's verses, under

the unwieldy title *Thou Shouldst Be Living at This Hour*, was brought out the following spring. It was reviewed here and there, and could be glimpsed, spottily, in the bookstores, but soon disappeared. My mother blamed this short shelf life on the miscalculation of a long-winded title; she took the trouble to inform me, with an uneasy sigh, that my father, who relied on her for much else, had insisted on it. When I dared to ask him what it meant, he rolled his eyes and puckered his bottom lip and said only that it was something out of Wordsworth anyone with a brain in her head ought to know. I had intended this mostly innocuous question as a preliminary breach into more dangerous territory: what I really hoped to hear was what my father thought of Alexander Alcott's incursion into Cyrus Alkana's inviolate precincts. I opened my mouth and nothing came out: I hadn't the courage to put it to him.

Instead I turned to my mother.

"He still doesn't know it was you," I accused. "Shouldn't he *know* who wrote that stuff?"

"If you tell him, my dear Sidney, I'll poison your cocoa," she said mildly. "And don't call it stuff, it's an appreciation. He understands it was the publisher who wanted it—the salespeople over there, for the noise it would make. Well, we've been *having* a bit of noise, haven't we? People are noticing—"

"But how can he *like* it? He can't like it, can he?"

"The idea of your father liking the likes of an Alexander Alcott, what a joke—he despises him, you've heard it yourself, those blistering letters, look how he keeps me up every night typing whatever's got stuck in his craw. Not that the ones to Alcott ever get into the mailbox."

"They don't?"

"And why should they? It wouldn't be politic, not when he's been so gracious and helped us out and done us a service. Listen, dearie," she said, "this Alcott's a rascal like the rest of them, and it gives your father no end of pleasure to see some fool of a charlatan come crawling on his knees, flattering and fawning away in that nice little preface of his."

"*Your* nice little preface—"

"That's only a quibble. Your father, wonderful man, takes it as a vindication and a surrender, and so do I—imagine, here's the venerated Alexander Alcott practically admitting that in the war between the Pure and the Sham, it's the Pure that carries the day."

She had flown into the Alkana sublime once again, and I could almost see the capital letters in the shine of her eyes.

There was no reviewer, meanwhile, who did not remark on the seeming anomaly of Alexander Alcott's exuberant praise for a sensibility so radically different from his own. The disparity was so glaring, the *Nation* admonished, that it could hardly have been inspired by collegial generosity—Alkana and Alcott were no more colleagues than they were brothers-in-arms, and it was an exceedingly strange pod that could contain two such unlike peas. This, it turned out, was to become the general theme: that a sophisticated artist imbued with the subtlest vibrations of the Zeitgeist had, inconceivably, lent his influence to the grotesque delusions of an archaist. The wonderment was so intense, and so confounding, that it brought on a second edition. The impetus for this miracle bubbled up, to start with, at those notorious dinner parties run by the literary set, a pack of up-to-date gossips (this was my mother's view) who followed the critics solely in order to tear into their arguments. From this narrowest of sanctums a wildfire of curiosity began to spread into the larger arena of the magazines: why had Alcott done it? And then: but *had* he done it? It was impossible, it made no sense, so vast a reputation stooping to crown with such extravagant laurels a negligible versifier—a mere mimic of the outmoded.

Outmoded? Cyrus Alkana spat out his grievance in phalanxes of rancor rushed off to the journals that spurned him. Did his assailants suppose they owned the language from the root up, and could do with it, by seigneurial right, whatever they wished? And what they wished to do with it, my father declaimed, was to pull off their shallow showy tricks—they said it themselves, straight out! These jabbering fakers mooing away at their slogans—make it new, break it down, chop it up, thin it out! And all of it morose, and ugly, and desolating, a wasteland! It wasn't only the language they were after, it was the tongue and the teeth and the eyeballs and the optic nerve itself, until they got all the way back into the human brain, to modernize even that.

Yet Cyrus Alkana was acquiring a faction of his own: he had his little coterie, his loyal little junta, the hot-blooded coven of his fans. The critic who had named him the American Keats now compared him to the school of Rembrandt, those ingenious disciples whose paintings, far from being imitations, "quaffed," he crowed, "from the selfsame celestial spring." How these accolades animated my mother! Praise for my father might be too sparse, or too bizarre, or too strenuously infatuated, but it satisfied her that after so many years in exile he had attained the recognition he had always deserved. It appeared not to trouble her that we still lived as thinly as we had before. My father may have arrived at a kind of fame, but even I could see that it came not so much from his devotees as from his detractors. The ongoing flood of those assaults on his enemies (you couldn't class it as correspondence, since there were never any answers) brought him, it developed, more notice from the reigning literati than whatever fading rumble was left of the shock of publication. There was no third edition. No one turned up to interview him. Occasionally the odd essay or two, like shards churned out of the dry soil of an abandoned dig, would crop up in this or that marginal journal. It might be a zealous study of the titular *Thou*—did it address the poet's soul, or the solitary reader, or the spirit of Wordsworth himself? Or else it would happen that Cyrus Alkana was cited in some university panel on forgotten minor figures.

In the two quiet years following what my mother happily went on calling my father's "apotheosis"—the flurry was long over—the deepest and most perplexing silence was the terrible muteness of Alexander Alcott. I had been wildly apprehensive all along. He had been the object of the minutest inquisitiveness; his repute had been usurped, even molested; some hinted at blackmail. And still he held his tongue. He made no mention of the abuse of his name. He wrote and spoke nothing in public or, as far as anyone could tell, in private. He raised no accusation or threat of anything remotely punitive. Week after week, month after month, I had been fearing a thunderclap: a dangerous letter, or the door bursting open, with police in pursuit. Again and again I badgered my mother—why was she so indifferent, how could she be so certain that there wouldn't be some sudden repercussion, a disgrace that might fall on us at any moment, and what would she do then?

"Oh, we're just fleas as far as he's concerned," she said, waving me off. "He doesn't take any notice, we're nothing to him, it would only be a comedown for the high-and-mighty Alexander Alcott to be bothered with us—"

"Is that why you took the risk? When you really don't know anything about him, the way he thinks, how he might take it—"

"How he might take it? You can see how he's taken it. He doesn't care. There never *was* a risk."

But another time she had a more deliberate argument.

"Did it ever occur to you," she began, "that the fellow might actually *admire* your father?"

"How could he? You're always saying they have nothing in common, they're opposites—"

"And out of opposition affinity grows. Suppose he's finally allowed himself a good look at what he said about your father—"

"What *you* said—"

"—and recognized the truth of it."

"The truth of what?"

"The truth of falling in love. A sort of conversion," she said, and here her voice, which was ordinarily excitedly soprano, darkened into a clairvoyant hush. "That's why he has nothing to complain of, he doesn't make a fuss, he leaves us alone. Because he's satisfied, because he *sees*. Because he *knows*."

I could only stare; there was nothing more to say. I was by now in my last year of high school, and had absorbed enough of her willfulness to recognize that this newest theory was as capricious as it was preposterous— the modernist Alcott suddenly smitten by the antiquarian

Alkana! And all of it resting on (what else could it be called?) a forgery. She had robbed him of his name; she stood ready to concoct his inmost sentiments. There was more at stake than my childhood notions had been able to swallow, when I was repeatedly told that my father was genuine and noble, and that his enemies weren't. And if proof was wanted, only see: my father's lines rhymed, and theirs didn't.

The next afternoon, when my father was again napping—his naps were becoming longer and more frequent—I put on my galoshes and walked through rapidly thickening snow to the public library. My arms were heavy with pretext: my mother, frugal as always, frowning on overdue fines, had instructed me that morning to return my father's latest batch of borrowed books, still piled on the radiator next to my bed. I was familiar with their hot smell, but had scarcely noticed their titles—the same hoary bards, the same sunsets and rivers and dryads, the same blurry infinities of a gods-infested cosmos. Except for the preoccupied librarian at the desk, who appeared to be sorting through files of index cards, the reading room was deserted and nearly silent; there was only the distant subterranean growl of the ancient furnace under our feet. The storm had done its work—I had the place to myself, and uninterrupted hours before me. And in this fortuitously secret space, below high windows palely lit and snow-muffled, I found the man I had come to look for: my father's enemy, my mother's dupe.

Or almost found him. The more I followed his tracings—he seemed to be everywhere—the more elusive he grew. Even so, you couldn't escape him. He took up whole chapters in one academic study after another, he proliferated in the bibliographies, and in the dictionaries he turned up between *alcohol* and *alcove*. Two or three essays in the serious journals attempted to uncover a venerable literary connection: was he a descendant of those estimable New England idealists, the Brook Farm Alcotts? Could he claim a cousinship, however distant, with the admirable Louisa May? There was no conclusive proof favoring a yes or a no; the genealogical paths were murky. None of this mattered to me; none of it counted. It was the living man I was after, so I burrowed into the glossy weeklies, into those "human interest" articles that confirm renown by adding to it. His name and his fame were titillating enough to land him there, among the politicians and movie stars—hadn't Eliot himself once filled a football stadium, declaiming before thousands of fans who'd never read a line? But Alexander Alcott disdained the public. He declined to be photographed. Yet as I leafed through mounds of mostly stale magazines I came on plenty of photos: in lieu of the poet, they were all, disappointingly, of the poet's house, taken from different angles. A modest stucco, set back from a countrified road. Rosebushes on either side of a door painted red.

Here and there, speculations seeped through—a marriage to an older widow who died; a speech hindrance, slight, intermittent, the cause of a raw self-consciousness. But these were only stories sprinkled among other stories. He lived alone. He was "reclusive," "reserved," "secretive." He "disliked leaving his house," though some could remember how, long ago, when he was still in his twenties, he had gone roaming together with other would-be young poets, scions of the new movement, to recite in parks and cafés. He was the only one to have lasted. The rest ended mainly as stockbrokers or insurance men; and two drank themselves to death. All these stories were sparse and uncertain. Was there a broken heart, a failed love? Of his childhood, I could discover nothing at all. It was as if he had been born out of a crater in the moon, and it gave me a chill to read that he was known to be irascible, a man with a heavy temper and a hidden grudge.—Or was it that the librarian, closing for the day, had already shut down the heat? It struck me as odd (I thought of my mother's cryptic affinity of opposites) that Alexander Alcott, exactly like my father, was unwilling to step past his own threshold; and that he too was easily roused to rage. A hollow equation: despite these echoing traits, Alcott was everywhere revered—he was in all the magazines!—while my father was more and more falling into eclipse.

By the time I got home, the snow had crept up to my ankles, and my mother was standing at the stove, stirring a pot. It was an unfamiliar scene. Her office had been dismissed earlier than usual. Even the neighboring sea lions had been herded indoors to avoid the rough weather.

She was quick to confront me. "Sidney!" The name itself was accusation; peevishly, she tugged at my wet sleeve. "Look at you, your hair all soaked through. What in the world have you been up to, what kept you so long?"

I had prepared a covering lie. When I told it, it sounded true. What need had my mother of the actual Alcott, when she so relished her moist inventions? And I hated the hobbling weight of my hair; she had forced me to let it grow to below my waist ("Pre-Raphaelite tresses," she said) to please my father.

"I got to looking through a bunch of college catalogues," I threw out, "and I think I've found just the place I want."

"And what place is that?"

On the spot I invented a name. "Kansas Polytech. For engineering."

"Girls can't be engineers," my mother said. "They won't let you, it's not any sort of normal occupation for a girl. Besides, who's going to pay for your room and board way off in some godforsaken nowhere? Not to mention the tuition, when right here you've got a perfectly fine city college that won't cost a penny—"

"You know my grades are good. I'll get a scholarship."

From his customary chair, his elbows lost in a surf of papers, my father growled, "Ah, let her go. The Bestowal's skipped her anyhow."

The Bestowal? I was past seventeen, sick of all such illusions, and more than ready to flee our moonbeam lives. It was math, it was physics, it was logic and dirt I was after, and brick and steel and cement—solid everyday things—and how a bridge can curve in the air like an arrow in flight, with seemingly nothing to keep it there. Some months afterward, I did in fact win a scholarship, not to some mythically faraway Kansas, but to an even more distant yet beckoning Texas: a full scholarship, together with a gratifyingly ample stipend. My mother in her melancholy letters never stopped insisting that I had been invited to study structural engineering at Texas A&M solely because of someone's mistaken impression that Sidney was a boy.

Until my father died nearly four years later, at the start of my last semester, I never went home again; I was glad to put half a continent between us. And then, as it happened, I was compelled to miss the funeral. A freak autumn blizzard followed by massive flooding had drowned Texan highways and railroad tracks, thwarting travel. My mother

sadly reported that there were only three at the graveside:
herself, the librarian from down the street, and the man
who had named my father the American Keats; it was he
who recited—*by heart*, my mother wrote—Cyrus Alkana's fourteen-stanza "Ode to the Aegean Cybele." She had
been lamenting my father's decline all along, week after
week, year after year: how the afternoon naps were now
beginning in the mornings (he was always tired), and how,
little by little, he had given up castigating his enemies—
because finally there were no more enemies. No one took
any notice, good or bad, of Cyrus Alkana: it had come
to that. There were no new verses. The Remington was
silent. The books languishing on the radiator, browning
at their margins, had become shockingly overdue, until
the librarian herself came to collect them. The heap of
folders on the farther end of the kitchen table remained
stagnant. "From a peak in Darien," my mother summed
up, "to the Slough of Despond." She had retired to care
for my father; she had a small pension.

There was no mention of Alexander Alcott. The name
and the incident had receded into worse than oblivion—
into a kind of caricature, an ephemeral embarrassment in
the long march of my mother's besotted loyalty to Cyrus
Alkana. Even the troubled shame her deceit had once
caused me, and my own childish terror of retribution, had
faded away. I was preoccupied now with weight-bearing
walls, I had begun designing simple beams and columns,

I was learning to calculate the load capacity of steel. In thrall to my slide rule and gravity's recalcitrance, I was—finally—freed from the lying romance of my father's house. To celebrate, I cut my hair very short, close to the scalp. In the mirror I saw the head of a boy. It pleased me to have acquired the look of a proper engineer. I tossed away my dresses and skirts, and took to wearing pants and rough shirts that buttoned the wrong way. In the campus cafeteria, crammed into a fifty-cent automatic photo booth, I sat for my portrait. With a mechanical click, a long row of boys' heads emerged from a slot. The most cheerful of the bunch I mailed to my mother. She never acknowledged it.

But when the floods had dried up and the rails were cleared, and my father had been in his grave for nearly a month, my mother wrote urgently again, begging me to come: what was to be done with his precious papers, his treasure trove, his golden egg, his soul's lantern, was it all to be condemned to perpetual night? Whom could she turn to for advice? She was helpless: the lone votary who had likened my father to Keats was useless for practical matters, not a thread or shred of any other literary connection remained, and only she and I were witnesses to the glory that lay in the scores of bulging folders she was daily uncovering in neglected corners and closets.

I dreaded those papers, and suspected her intent. Surely she didn't suppose that I would gaze, admire, and at last be swept away—what was the Aegean Cybele to me? She knew my detachment. Or did she imagine (and what might my mother *not* imagine?) that I could somehow lead her to certain grandly monumental Texan libraries eager to enshrine Cyrus Alkana's hallowed archive? I was, despite all, an authentic Alkana—of the bloodline if not of the Bestowal. She meant to lure me back, to draw me in—to keep me imprisoned in that dank emptiness that was just now invading my lungs as I climbed the stairs to my parents' old flat. It was no more than a ruse, this implausible commotion over my father's papers: I was to be his surrogate, her stay against Cyrus Alkana's extinction.

The grimy fake marble steps and the iron balustrade with its rusting scrolls were the same as they had always been. The shrunken hallways and dusky stairwells groaned out their old echoes. Even the smell of the place was everything I remembered—a sour fume of changelessness, defeat, aging. Silence and loneliness. Two flights above (I had by now arrived at the third-floor landing) a muddy wash of voices swelled and ebbed—and then I heard the shutting of a door, and downward footsteps.

I looked up, and looked again; I stood where I was. Through the gaps in the railings I saw a man descending. One hand slid lightly along the banister, the other gripped a fedora. He was moving easily, firmly, confident of his tread. He wore a long tweed coat with a velvet collar. His shoes were impeccable, the leather unscuffed, the laces orderly. On the fourth landing, glancing below, he hesitated, startled; clearly he had expected the way to be unobstructed. But I stood where I was, taking him in. I recognized the ruddy mass of his hair, the color now much subdued, the wilderness of it tamed and civilized. He had grown a pinkish mustache, overrun by white, that oddly hid his upper lip. As he came nearer, I caught the tilt of his left eye listing toward an ear, like a skiff about to capsize—but his gait was strong, he was robust all over, and he passed me by with a stranger's nod. My tongue felt frozen in my mouth. How could he know me, with my boy's head, and my pants and borrowed lumberjacket?

It was my father. I had never before seen him so well-dressed.

Ruse! Deceit! Lie! The pretext of his papers? No, the unthinkable, the heinous: my mother the trickster! Had she concocted his decline and his dying, and all of it to snatch me back?

I took the last two flights at a gallop, and faced the door that would open into the life I had repudiated—that enervated life of mist and chimera. Into the scarred lock I thrust the old key my mother had pressed on me long ago. It had taught me to be surreptitious.

She was standing at a window, looking into the street below—watching, I thought, my father go. But where? And in a coat with a velvet collar! When she turned, alerted by the cat's squeal of the doorknob, I saw how the skin of her jaw hung loose, and how sparse, nearly naked, her eyebrows had become: it gave her a worn abandoned stare.

But her voice was lively. "Oh, what a pity, such a pity," she sang out. "Here you are, and you've just missed him." And then: "Sidney! Your hair, what have you done to yourself? Just look at you, what a getup, I couldn't believe that photo, how your father would be appalled—"

She spoke as if the years of my absence had all at once dissolved, as if my having just then materialized was no more than a daily commonplace.

But I would not allow her to distract me. "You made me come back," I said: bitterly, coldly. "And all for nothing."

"For nothing? If only you'd got here on time! He sent a note ahead—it went to the publisher, so it was delayed almost a week, it turned up only day before yesterday, and by then you'd left, you were on the train for sure, there was no way I could let you know. How I wish you had seen him!"

"Let me know?" I could catch hold only of the tail of this whirlwind. "I did see him," I said. "On the stairs, coming down, he didn't recognize me—"

"Condolences, he called it. But Sidney, it was so much more, and imagine, Alexander Alcott right in this very *spot*! In this very room!"

A rush of shame; the fury drained out of my throat. She was pulling at my sleeve—her old proprietary habit—and I followed where she led. Was she the captive of a delusion? She was ill, her senses were deteriorating, she believed my father was dead, and not five minutes ago I had seen him alive! And hale! And in a coat with a velvet collar! And worse, horrifyingly worse: she had mistaken him for his most hated antagonist.

The kitchen table was littered with remnants of a repast: empty teacups and lavish little colored cakes of a kind that had never before appeared in our household. A sugar bowl where once stood a perpetual bottle of ink. The Remington too gone from its place, as if a cavity had been carved out of the air.

"You see," she said, "he even brought me these pretty petit fours, that's how gentlemanly he was! And he told me things I never knew, things your father kept to himself—"

It was brutal to listen to. I could think of nothing to say to these muddles, and while she went to find another cup for me (she filled it with weak tea grown cold), I looked all around, searching for evidences of my father: some vagrant sheet with his obsessive scratchings, an ink-stained pamphlet with a note stuck in it, his coddled old dipping pen. There were only the bare plates and their pink-and-yellow crumbs.

"I always understood it was Cain and Abel between

those two," she went on, "but I never dreamed they'd been so young, boys no more than fifteen or so, hotheads, a falling-out like that, and even now it isn't clear who was Cain and who was Abel, except that he had that lip all covered up—"

It was unendurable. I broke in headlong: "*What* boys, for God's sake what *is* it! And where was he going just now, he never used to bother about a hat—"

"Oh Sidney, don't be so dense"—her old tone. "Can't you see how remarkable it is? That he *came*? That he was here? He saw the obituary, a tiny little thin thing, no more than six lines, it didn't at all add up to your father's proper stature, but still, the blood between them—"

"Blood? What are you saying?"

"The blood of the Alkanas. That's what brought him."

She told me then what she admitted she had always known: it was my father's great secret, she said, he had never once spoken of it, and she had never violated what she perceived to be a sacred ban—a ban rooted in an insatiable rage; or in guilt; or in shame. Or perhaps even in fossilized indifference. But she had known his secret for years, and had, in truth, known more of it than he knew himself.

All this I submitted to with a skepticism mixed with fear: what fraud was she brewing now? The purposeful drama of it, her small pale eyes theatrically effulgent, where was she intending to take me?

"I saw him just that one time," she said, "on Bleecker Street, down a staircase into a smoky cellar, candles set in saucers, a dozen chairs in a circle, that sort of place. A reading along with two others, vile simpleminded stuff, red wheelbarrows and chickens, he didn't read well at all, and he had that little notch over his mouth. He was already calling himself by that pretentious name he took on, not that it had any shine to it then. But I knew right away."

It was as if she was drawing me on with tightening straps, and where was she taking me?

I asked, "What did you know?"

"The hidden thing. That my husband had a brother."

And again, cautiously: "How could you know that? If you never saw him before?"

"Because of the resemblance. Except for that notch. And when I got home that night I never told your father any of it."

The illogic, the waywardness! The fantasy, the delusion!

I surrendered docility and tore into her wildly. "You ran into someone years ago who looked a little like my father and you decided he was my father's brother—"

"What a fool you are, you have no imagination, you don't understand, you can't *see*! There wasn't an iota of difference, every cell of him, every grain and pore of him, every hair on his head! Identical! And that's the one the world adores, not your father, they throw garlands around his neck . . . how your father despised that man, and he had no inkling . . ."

Her face collapsed into its grooves, and it came to me—heavily, grievously, ruinously—that my mother's trick was not of this moment. It was lifelong. My father and his dithyrambs were dead, obliterated, and the man in the coat with the velvet collar was his enemy, whom the world had wreathed in garlands.

But still she was dogged, and it spiraled out, the maelstrom of it, Cain and Abel, Jacob and Esau . . . Cyrus and Alexander, all of them twinned in the womb, contending even there. And then the falling-out, the horrid divide, that delta of flesh cut out of a lip, the outcry, the blood . . . "You can't really get a good look at it," she said, "a bit of a slash, like a sewed-up harelip, it was only one of those little pocketknives, an argument between boys, that's what he was telling me—"

An argument between boys? Prodigious boys, extraordinary boys, boys who were already preserving their verses in packets tied with knotted string, wondrous and singular boys, though doubled by the bloodline of the Alkanas; and it was over the bloodline of the Alkanas that they fought: whether it was destined to course through the cosmos or through a grain of sand, whether it was to be venerable and honored or new-made and radical, whether it was sunk in overgrown ancient scum or alive in the pulse of the modern . . . even then, even then, in their teens! Not over a skate or a pair of purloined socks, or whatever trivial spats ordinary boys turn into wars. The knife that sliced the lip might easily, by a finger's length, have pierced eye or throat—his brother's knife, captured and wielded by your father. One boy owned the knife, the other used it. The intent to maim, mutual. The rage, mutual. How alike they were, striving for supremacy! And then he ran away, your father, the almost-murderer, the runaway criminal who might so easily have blinded his brother, or killed him . . .

My mother recited these passionate claims with a strained breathlessness, while I, disbelieving, shocked into ridicule, went on numbly stirring my tepid tea. "Are you telling me—did *he* tell you—that it was a fight over—what a piece of nonsense—*style*?"

"You stupid engineer!" she cried out. "All you have any feeling for is dust—bricks, concrete, who knows what you're after, looking like that, and you a born Alkana! It was the Bestowal, it was your father fighting against the tide to have his life! Even then he would never go with the tide, don't you see? And in spite of it, when it comes to the marrow of things, there's not a droplet's difference between them . . . Do you know why that man came today? Do you understand why?"

"No," I said.

"And just think how worried you once were, how afraid you were that he'd punish us—"

"It was long ago," I said.

"I knew he'd never harm us. I always knew it."

"You stole his name, you abused him."

"Oh, his name! He gave up his name, didn't he? He got rid of it—not to be tainted by his brother, his derided brother, his brother the . . . *archaist*." The word was ruthless: she trickled out a covetous little laugh, half pain, half victory. "It was his fame I stole. For your father's sake, to catch the world's eye, to get him into print. But I knew," she breathed out grandly, "he'd never harm us."

"My father was harmed. You made him a butt."

"You're hard on me, aren't you—when all my life I've been a person of forbearance. I never let on to your father that the man he most detested carried his own blood in his veins."

"His blood, his veins! How could you *not* expect some retaliation—at least a protest? How could you not? You gave out a hundred different reasons—"

"There was only one reason."

Again the tightening straps; the reins were now wholly in her hands.

I asked, "And what was that?"

"He didn't mind. It's exactly the thing he came to tell me. That he didn't mind, he'd never minded. And I always trusted that he wouldn't. Because," she persisted, "they were breast to breast even before they were born."

She stopped and looked me over; her nostrils danced in wary distaste. I saw that she was judging me less by what she took to be my indecency of feeling than by my shorn boy's head.

When I left her—she didn't try to keep me, after all—I understood that my guileless mother would go on believing forever in the binding force of the bloodline of the Alkanas. And I made no further move to dispute it.

It was the librarian from down the street who salvaged my father's papers. They were stored in the library's cavernous underground—one hundred and twenty-three cardboard boxes of unsorted manuscripts, some typed, many more handwritten in the blue-black ink he favored—*awaiting*, my mother wrote in the last letter I ever had from her, *the unborn critic who will restore him to his rightful peers*. But when some years later a nearby water main burst and inundated the old building's outmoded electrical and heating systems, the library had to be demolished (no engineer would touch it), washing away what a very few still revere as Cyrus Alkana's lordly if unsung art.

A Hebrew Sibyl

My mother was a native of this place, though my father, a trader in pots, was not. Each year, usually in the spring, he came from his home country to buy the wares of our region. He would remain with us, if the weather and the sea's temper held, into the last days of summer. He spoke our language well, and could read and write in our alphabet. Still, the kiln masters, who could not, called him *barbaros*, and laughed at his clumsiness with our easy "th." The lekythoi flasks, for instance, he pronounced "lekydoi"; it made him sound childish. Behind his back he was resented and disliked, even as he brought us prosperity.

It was my father's practice to choose the pots he intended to purchase at the very moment they were taken from the kilns and set out on wooden slats to cool. He did this with a certain harsh and almost contemptuous speed; he knew instantly what wouldn't do, never mind that to any ordinary eye the skyphos or krater he spurned as imperfect might be altogether indistinguishable from those he deemed flawless. And then, after the favored pots were wrapped in linen strips and cushioned in straw and sent on to the port town in a procession of donkey carts, they would be filled (so my father explained to me) with oils and syrups and perfumes of a kind not to be found in his own land. Yet not all: only those vessels designed for freight. The others, prized solely for their beauty, were destined, he said, for the tables of scholars and aristocrats.

There was still another reason my father was derided, this one far more grave than his foreigner's tongue. He was a confessed atheist. It was on this account that my mother had no communal standing as his wife, and was subjected to unkind whisperings: she was called concubine, bond-maid, helot; and sometimes, to my shame, harlot. My father had refused the customary marriage rites under the aegis of Hestia, to whose favor my mother had been dedi-cated at birth, and whose chapel was one of the grandest. When I was old enough to go about by myself, I often wandered there, to stand between the gilded pilasters and stare upward at her image. I went alone; I was always alone. Like my mother, I was not wholly shunned—our polis was too orderly for something so noticeably offen-sive. Instead, we were discreetly, almost politely, avoided. But here, in the goddess's dim cool shrine, Hestia's arms, outstretched as if ready to embrace, seemed welcoming, even as they overawed with their stony weight. A fire was kept burning in a brazier in her vast lap, tended by a very young acolyte, a boy my own age, dressed like the priests in a pleated white tunic fringed at the ankles. With each shudder of the tossing flames, the goddess's breasts flashed like bucklers; shadows wavered over her massive round toes. And then, as I looked on steadily, her eyes with their carved pupils shifted her gaze to me. I saw that she knew me for what I was: the outcome of my mother's humiliation and my father's subversion.

But my father was insouciant, scorning whatever reached us of these disparagements. And in the months he was with us, we were happy. He had built for us a fine large house, rather more plain than ostentatious; somehow, not because of its size but because of my father's presence, it signified wealth. Indoors, the walls were stippled with brilliant frescoes, landscapes thickened by fruit-bearing orchards, and skies rife with colorful birds. He had forbidden the usual scenes from the lives of the gods; there were to be no gods in our house. My mother protested, but vaguely. She was uncommonly compliant, especially when he teased and kissed her. He called her his camelopard: she had a long neck, on which her small head turned silkily, eyeing him as if to fix him in place. Her tentative smile darkened when the sun's slant began to hint at autumn and his nearing departure. She had been no more than seventeen, one of many earthquake orphans under the care of the polis, when he found her. Though by then seven years had passed, she was still in mourning for her parents. She had seen them devoured by a black crevice widening and widening, out of which a wild fang of blaze leaped up to snatch them, two living torches, into the ravenous abyss. My reticent mother rarely spoke of this, and when she did, it was with a shiver of obeisance, I hardly knew to whom. The gods, the priests, our sibyl? The *barbaros* who had inexplicably succored her, and given her shelter and the child who was to become his delight?

That I was my father's delight I was fully confident. I was his delight, and his darling, and his joy; and also his little sparrow, and his pearl, and his pomegranate, and his garden of love. These were his fanciful names for me, and many more. He made me believe (and for a long time I did believe it) that he came every year not to see to his business at the kilns, but solely to marvel at how much I had grown, and to bring me presents of woven bracelets and pendants of polished stone and necklaces strung with beads that were really the shells of tiny sea creatures. He told me of the great fishes that swam singing and sighing alongside his ship, huge monstrous things with hairy fins and glistening eyes, and of how when it stormed in the night the waves turned into thrashing tongues frothing at the lips of prow and stern; and that he bore these queer perils all for the sake of once again taking into his arms his little sparrow, his darling, his garden of love, his only delight.

And then would begin my father's anxious questioning: what did I like best to eat? And why did I refuse wine? Where were my playmates, why was I so often alone? Why did I leave my mother, only to loiter among the chapels? What did I do there?

I answered dutifully but aslant. How could I admit, as I stood ringed by the sweetness of his embrace, that my father was the cause of our isolation? Though he periodically engaged a number of household servants, as soon as he departed they would instantly vanish. During the long months of his absence, my mother wrapped herself in loneliness. No one came to us. In a corner, on a little lion-footed tripod table covered with a woolen cloth, she kept an image of Hestia, her protectress. It was carved out of cedar and no taller than her forearm. In the spring, as my father's return approached, she hid it away. Even I, who lived within the sound of her thin breathing, hardly knew where. All this because my father was *atheos*, and we carried his stain—my mother less than I. It was I who carried his blood.

What I dared not tell was how I came to fear the taste of wine. My mother and I drank clear water with our meals, but often enough our cups held wine mixed with water, a faintly half-sweet, half-bitter flavor that, chiefly in the depth of summer, I swallowed greedily. My father, oddly, always avoided our wine, even when it was much diluted. And he had another strange refusal: with a quick thrust of his hand he declined all bread, whether wheat or barley—but only for a certain set of eight days; and after that he would eat normally. My mother did not question these incomprehensible omissions. It was how they lived in his home country, she told me, where even the bread and the wine were unlike our own.

But now I could no longer endure the taste or look or smell of wine. I would not touch any cup that had once held so much as a drop of it. The faintest vinous aroma, even at a distance, struck me as ominous, redolent of the terror that had inflamed me one melancholy afternoon, after my mother and I had said our farewells to my father. The air, with its memory of last year's abandonment, had already begun to grow sick with its presentiments of loneliness. My father clasped each of us close, confiding, to my mother especially, assurances of future comforts, and nestling my face in the familiar bristle of his beard; yet I could see in his eyes that his thoughts were more of departure than of far-off arrival. All that morning he had been supervising the noisy loading of the caravan, while the donkeys yawped amid their droppings, and the drivers abused one another with friendly curses. The moment the last cart was out of sight, my mother's waning smiles flattened into the cheerless silence that would, I knew, afflict her for many weeks.

And so I fled into the late-summer heat, and went to walk again among the chapels. My mother was glad to have me go; I understood that she meant to take out from its hiding place, unobserved, the diminutive image of her protectress, and would set beside it the ritual dishes of figs and sacred seeds. It puzzled me how so shrunken a figure could claim to hold equal power with the towering Hestia in the grandeur of her proper shrine, but my mother's belief was steadfast. As water will flow into any vessel prepared to receive it, she instructed me, so must the presence of the goddess flow into her material incarnation, no matter if it is no bigger than a hand's breadth . . . *ouai*, she murmured, if only your father would not deny it!

Secretly I was tempted to deny it too, and as I stole into the dusk of Hestia's chapel (always it was my single-minded destination), and saw at the far end of its shrouded nave the goddess's mighty lineaments, my mother's tiny replica seemed no more than a childish toy. I had come out of desire, and also out of fear; I feared my father's denial, and my own. Yet by now my father was irretrievably gone, my mother was sick at heart, and in the hallowed twilight of that place I felt sheltered by the force and majesty of the goddess's brooding head and broad thighs, those marble hills in whose valley rested the sacred fire. All things were small beside her, my unhappy mother smaller still.

The acolyte was not alone. A woman stood before

the altar at Hestia's feet. She was neither young nor old, her waist was thick and round as a pumpkin, and she was pouring a dark syrup from a narrow flask into the swirling well of the libation bowl. The dense liquid fell in waves and folds, and when the flask was emptied, she placed next to the bowl a barley cake that smelled of honey. The acolyte held out a rattling cup. The woman dropped in a drachma and hurried away.

I distrusted this boy. He was dressed like the priests, but he was not a priest; he was only a boy.

"You always come," he said. I had never before heard his voice; it was the voice of a female child. Was it because he was not permitted to speak, and could not remember how? I watched him as he sidled to the altar to tend to his duty there—was he not the goddess's servant? But instead he broke off a bit of the cake and licked the beads of honey seeping out.

"Want some?" he said in his strange squeal. "It's for the priests, though."

"Are you allowed?"

He gave me a sly look. "They won't know, will they?"

He picked up a ladle and dipped it into the libation bowl. I saw him sip, and sip again. The wine shimmered and shook in its krater, and then it glinted and shuddered at the rim of the ladle. I was all at once ravished by an invincible thirst; on this parched day of my father's leave-taking, I had forgotten food and drink. I took in the smell,

a wild and sour stench, as of some small animal's dung. It
was the spoor of the wine, and the wine was in the ladle,
trembling there, moving closer, until a droplet touched
my lip and wet my tongue, when the stench turned all at
once deliriously sweet, like butterflies liquefied, or bird-
beaks pounded into flowery powder, and I drank, deeply,
thirstily, drivenly, a violator, a betrayer of the priests
and the goddess herself, but I was indifferent, my throat
was a vine on fire, my fingers crawled like twisted vines,
vines charred white coiled round all my parts, I was alone,
alone, swept up by a burning whirlwind and thrown into
an airless void, I belonged nowhere, and I was afraid,
afraid of the flame between the goddess's thighs, afraid of
my lips and my tongue and the smoldering coals that were
my eyes; and I was afraid of what I suddenly and terribly
knew.

It was a long time before I could return to that place.
When I did, the acolyte kept his distance. He never again
spoke to me.

And when my father had been gone for several weeks,
and we were in our customary seclusion, my mother one
day confided to me, all unexpectedly, what she had long
understood to be my father's secret. It was only because
of the earthquake that he had taken her, she told me, an
orphan tainted by the wrath of Hades, and it was because
of the earthquake that she was not the proper wife of a
proper husband, and was made to suffer now like some

grieving widow, though she was not a widow, and what was she then, if she was not a proper wife? My mother's recurrent malaise too often plagued our solitude, and I saw that she was again falling into forlornness. It was her habit to skirt any talk of the cataclysm that had despoiled her earlier years, particularly when I was nearby to hear it; she wished to shield me from these old scenes, even if in their remoteness from our ordinary landscape they seemed to me no different from fables. Yet now, in the fever of her telling (it came upon her like a seizure), she spoke over and over of the wrath of Hades whose punishment it was, the ruination of houses and orchards and animals and crops, the ruination of everything civilized, and how in the bleak aftermath of the last of the tremors she had lingered for many hours half-naked in her torn tunic at the brink of the steaming trench; and she told of the looting that followed, and the riots when there was little to eat, and the knives and the fury and the bloodshed. The wrath of Hades? All this impressed me as a passing figment of her disordered temper: how did such long-ago wounds accord with our sedate and harmonious polis, governed by the priests under the inspiration of our sibyl? And had not those wounds been transfigured by the newcomer to our restrained and measured realm, my mother's savior, the redeemer of her misfortunes—my father?

"And did I not know it," she wailed, "did I not know it even then? He comes and he comes, but one time he will not come, the sea will break his vessel, he will stop his breath among the fishes, or else, or else," in a voice almost too thin to grasp, "one day he will not come because he no longer wishes to come."

I asked why my father, who loved me so, would not ever wish to come.

And then my mother confessed what she believed to be my father's great deceit. In his home country, she told me, he had a proper wife, how could it be otherwise? And a proper family, and yes, a foreign daughter, how could it be otherwise?

I believed her belief. I believed it even more intently than I believed her belief in the dark god's spite: how should my guileless mother merit the lash of his under-world? But the other daughter, how my envious imaginings stung! Did she love my father as yearningly as I? It rankled me that a foreign girl could bask under his fond eye nearly all the year, while me he held close only for a summer's blink. And did she not speak his home-country tongue, as I could not, and was she not intimate with his home-country ways? How often and often had I wished that my father were one of us!—though sometimes, as I contemplated my mother pleading before her protectress's small shrine, it came to me that the other daughter might be no more than a phantom, the lurking creature of my mother's frights.

But when my father returned, all these darknesses

fled. His ship had skimmed a stormless sea, he was hale and ruddy-cheeked from the prickly northern winds, and oh! the presents he brought, brooches inlaid with turquoise, and baskets woven in many colors heaped with gleaming olives different in shape and taste from ours, and scarves and bracelets and a glossy bronze looking-glass, and even sandals hung with silver beads, unlike any we had ever seen. My mother brightened; her toy Hestia had already been rushed into its hiding place. Immediately fresh troops of servants were bustling everywhere, sweeping out neglected corners, crisscrossing the courtyard, fetching water and grinding meal, all the while showing uncommon deference. It was easy then to put away jealousy: how plain it was that my father could *not* love a foreign child more than he loved his pearl, his pomegranate, his little sparrow!

And now we were happy once more. In the mornings my father went to the kilns, and again in the late afternoon, but the hours in between belonged to my mother and me. Together we set out for the fields, carrying pouches of cakes and fruit. We walked until the footpaths ended and everything before us was brush and tangles of green, and then my father would be sure to tell us that the fields of his own land were no different; it was only the families of wildflowers that were not the same. Or else, to flavor our lavish dinners of fish or lamb, we would visit the market stalls in the agora, in search of herbs and spices he was familiar with and we were not. My father would sometimes allow me to go with him to the kilns before sunset, to tally and mark with his mark the pots he had purchased that day. The tedium and the dust and the heat and the incessant shouting of the kiln masters, he warned, would tire me. But despite the lingering smoke and the biting smells of glaze and moist clay, I was never wearied there, where the armies of finished pots marched in brilliant rows—how I loved to see their shapes and colors! Some had handles like ears, and others were thin-necked and fat-bellied, and on their flanks so many patterns, scrolls or stripes or leaves curled like snails.

Even so, what enchanted me more than all the rest were the pots that told stories: figures in motion, bearing kraters or kneeling or with uplifted arms gripping weapons, all devotedly and meticulously painted, as if they could come alive if only they willed it. Like any child of our polis, I knew their stories well: here was Gaia, here was Poseidon with his trident, and Demeter and Zeus, and poor frightened Persephone, dragged by deathly Hades into the chasm's cruel gullet. And still my father coveted them all!

For the very first time I dared to question him. Hadn't he banned from the fresh walls of our new-built house any fresco depicting the gods, no matter how it would have pleased my mother, whose every solace he unfailingly sought to indulge? And now look—all these sanctified chronicles on pots, and as always he intended to take them away with him!

My father caressed my cheeks, a tender habit meant to calm me, though now it could not. "Oh my little bird," he said, "only see how beautiful, the tunics of the women, how the cloth folds and unfolds, like shadow and light, and the limbs of the men, their force—"

"But they are *gods!*" I cried. Could he not see, did he not know?

"In my home country they will not be gods, they will be what they are, beautiful mortal men and beautiful mortal women."

And I thought: how barren, how deprived, was my father's far-off land, where beauty was denied to the gods.

It was after this troubled colloquy (and wasn't it almost a quarrel?) that my father began to ply me with strange tales. They were, he said, the history of his home country. We would rest in the courtyard in the thick of the afternoon, when the air quivered from heat, and the pavement sizzled, and the servants dozed over their tasks, and my mother napped in the shuttered cool of an inner room. Then my father told of an infant saved from drowning by a king's daughter, who reared him to grandeur in the royal palace, only to see him lead a fearsome rebellion. He told of a youth who knew the meaning of dreams, whose envious brothers sold him into a foreign kingdom, where he rose out of a dungeon to become a powerful vizier. He told of a great flood that swallowed the earth, except for one old drunkard with his one small boat, who salvaged all future life. He told of an ill-starred voyager, who, thrown overboard by terrified sailors, fell into the belly of a mammoth fish. He told of a boy who brought down a giant with nothing more formidable than a simple slingshot.

My father told all these stories, and many more. Some I shrank from and some I wondered at; but privately I judged them inferior—what were they, after all, but the earthbound dry happenings of the ordinary world, haplessly cut off from the dazzlements of Olympus? Men, not gods, struggled in these tales, while *our* histories, how glorious they were!—the rages and lusts and jealousies of goddesses and gods, how they caused the skies to rumble and the seas to churn, how the lot of humankind hung from their passions, and how, if they were drawn to the love of a mortal, what heroes, Heracles and Achilles, erupted from their loins!

I said nothing of this to my father.

Instead, I asked whether in his home country they kept a sibyl, as we did.

No, my father said. And I began to pity him a little: it seemed to me then that my father, *barbaros* and *atheos*, must live in an uncivilized land. This dim inkling of a divide, finer than a spider's line, made me cling to him all the more, and to the everyday pleasures of our little family.

We went on wandering the fields, the three of us, often lying contented and laughing in the long grasses with our heads flattening the wildflowers, and our noses yellowed by pollen, and our mouths purpled from the juice of the grapes we had eaten. And still—though he was not, he did not wish to be, one of us—I was my father's darling, his sparrow, his pomegranate, his garden of love.

But I determined that I would no longer go walking among the chapels, and that the great gleaming Hestia in her cathedral shrine would never again lure me.

Year after year, unwaveringly, I kept this private vow, both when my father was happily with us and in the dreary months of my mother's melancholia when he was not. There were seasons that brought him to us in the earliest days of spring, and other times when summer had already reached its midpoint. All this fickleness rested, he teased, on the temperament of the sailors: an indolent crew dallies and dawdles. Or if the big fishes knock their heavy tails against the starboard, like cats begging for a morsel. But we knew he meant the whims of the hungering sea.

One year, when the summer was beginning to drift toward exhaustion, my father had still not come.

"It must be the winds," I said, "flying hard against him."

Or I said, to lighten my mother's thoughts, "How lazy those sailors are."

Or I said, "The sea cats are crowding his path."

And then I said, "Surely he will come, he always comes, soon he will come, he has never not come—"

But my mother said, "He will not come."

And he did not.

From then on, my mother descended into grieving. We were invariably alone. Our suppers were meager. Morning and evening I heard my mother's murmured pleas and lamentations before her small protectress, now always out of its hiding place; but the propitiatory dishes were bare.

"*Ouai*," she soughed, "he is drowned, he is drowned," and covered the twist of her mouth with her pale hands, on which I could see the gray ridges of veins like the ridges made by cart tracks in earth after rain.

Or else she said in her flat strained voice, "He has chosen his proper family, it is his proper place."

And was this not, I thought, the very reason for the fierceness of our love? Because he was not, and did not wish to be, one of us—and yet had he not come to succor and rejoice us?

But my mother said bitterly, "It was only for the kilns that he came, and never for us. Never did he come for us."

And I saw that grief was coarsening and muddling my mother's heart. She was willing now, more and more, to speak of the earthquake, and of the wild time afterward, those fearful years of chaos and violence, as dire as the upheaval itself. She told and retold (how tedious it was!) the old familiar tales of how the priests in despair had summoned our sibyl from the far north, and how they kept her secluded, no one knew where—grove, or cave, or forest—and how through the sway of her divinations and prophecies our polis was at length pacified and cleansed. These storied events had neither impressed nor dismayed my father; the sibyl, he would chide my mother, was mere woman, and many women were wise who never governed . . . and then my mother would clasp her breast as if a tiny beast were strangling there, and cry out, "*Ouai, atheos!*"

In those sorrowful days of mourning, my father's erasure from our lives returned to her awry: it was the earthquake that had devoured him, and never the sea; or she would fall into a dreamy lassitude and promise that my father was certain to come again when the sun burned hot on the lintel and flocks of foreign birds filled the skies. And sometimes, because I gave no obeisance to her little Hestia, and passed it by without so much as a glance, she charged me with denying the gods, and turned her plaintive look on me to ask, "Who will there be to marry one such as you?"

In this way, half-bewildered and maundering, my mother sickened. She vomited the gruel I pressed on her and spat out the water in her cup, and the skin of her neck frayed like a wrinkled rope, and in the spring, when my father once more did not come, she died. Season after season, month upon month, time relentlessly dividing itself, I sat solitary in my father's house (so I regarded it), and saw the pavement in the courtyard crack, and a wilderness of scrub creep up through a mazy map of fissures, and watched as the frescoes faded and flaked into a drizzle of powder at a finger's touch.

But I had not forgotten the hoard of my treasures—my father's countless gifts of brooches and necklaces and pendants and bracelets, each with its precious stones, and the sandals with their silver beads, too beautiful to have ever been worn, and the bronze looking-glass. I had long ago given up adorning myself; these things were useless to me now. One by one, I took them to the agora to sell, lest I become impoverished. It was only the bronze looking-glass that I thought to keep.

I disliked these periodic excursions to the market stalls, infrequent though they were. The sharp smell of spices pierced and saddened me: here our little family had once loitered, while my father sorted through ruffled leaves and roots and tubers and tubs of ground bark with the same determined delicacy he brought to choosing lekythoi at the kilns, as if a sprig of fenugreek was as lovely to his eye as a painted jar. But now, caught among the roiling streams of tattle that agitated the agora, I knew myself to be a rumor, a byword, a warning; yet I hardly understood why. Was I not as native to our polis as any passerby? The stares of the merchants unsettled me—they retreated into the dark of their stalls as I approached. Was it because I was a woman alone, an abandoned relic in a hollow ruin, childless, unwanted? Was it because I rarely cared to speak? To whom should I speak, and to what end? Who would love me as I had once been loved by my father?

In the bronze looking-glass I saw what I was. My father's eyes gazed back at me with unfamiliar ferocity; swollen blue-black pockets bulged beneath them. My hair, white as a cloud, unbound and untamed, was as vagrant as some massive shrub torn up by an unforgiving wind. My mouth frightened me: a hive of terrible silences.

In my fifty-seventh year, long after even the looking-glass had been sold, our sibyl died. Very few could remember a time when she was not the unseen guardian of our decorum and our laws; for us, she was ageless and faceless. Her lineage was unknown. No one had ever heard her voice. It was said that the goddess to whom she was pledged had decreed at her birth that she was not to live beyond two hundred years.

And soon a savage tumult seized our polis. Bins of ripened fruits overturned and trampled in the marketplace, stalls barricaded, old women wailing in the confusion. Menacing packs of youths heaving boulders downhill, to crash into whatever stood in their path. Thieves running free, hauling their prey. Trembling curs prowling in the night, sniffing for scraps, the tattered fur hanging loose from their bellies. Everywhere fear—fear of brokenness, fear of hunger, fear of bloodletting and malice.

Only I was left unharmed, I with my snarled coils of hair, my speech idled and shattered, sitting day after day under the lintel of my father's decaying house, listening to the groans and maledictions of a dying polis. Fires on the hills, fires in the fields, the chapels on fire, the agora smoldering, always the fires: the sun veiled in smoke.

It was on just such an afternoon of burning air that the priests came. I saw them at first at a distance, a procession of seven shrouded figures, and supposed it to be yet another rite of expiation to stem the crawling flames. I had often witnessed these futile parades as they passed, chanting and swinging their censers, as if those small vessels of heated coals had the power to extinguish the greater conflagration. As they moved nearer, they were more easily defined: all wore long pleated white garments fringed at the anklebone and flecked with soot. Six were bare-headed and clean-shaven; two of these were clearly acolytes in their teens, and one was a withered patriarch with a palsied chin. The seventh, whom I took to be their chief, wore a gilded circlet round his head, and plaited through his abundant beard were sooty ribbons of colored silk.

But this time there were no censers, and no chanting, and the silent cortege drifted unfathomably toward me, until it stopped directly before my feet.

One of the acolytes knelt and removed my sandals. At a word from the priest with the palsied chin—who appeared to be their spokesman, though not their leader— the other invaded the dirty gloom of my father's house and quickly brought out my mother's toy Hestia. Her little shrine had remained in its old corner, untouched and untended; but the lion-footed table that held it I had long ago sold.

I was instructed to follow where I was led, past the blighted agora into fields of grasses like blackened straw, and onward through soot-blasted fields farther yet, where my father had never taken us, and over a rise and beyond it, and finally into a place of stones. Here the fires had never reached. I was made to walk on my naked feet, so that they might toughen and grow hard and invulnerable, no matter that the thistles were piercing my heels, or that my soles were torn and bloodied. The stones rose tall and taller as we proceeded, until they seemed to form a kind of grotto, a cavern of earth and stone through which ran a trickle of icy water. I was shown the nearby spring that was its source: I was permitted to drink of this spring, and to relieve myself there, but it was forbidden to bathe in its water, except for when the moon was shrunk to the shape of a fingernail. It was forbidden to forage for leaves or berries: I must be satisfied with what, morning and evening, the acolytes would bring. If it turned cold, I was not to plead for a fire; again I must be content with whatever habit or vesture the acolytes might offer. It was forbidden to speak to the acolytes. It was forbidden to cover my feet; it was an offense to the gods. It was forbidden to depart from this place; it was a profanation. It was forbidden to eat or drink on the days designated for the coming of the priests: my body must be purified in preparation.

These were the precepts imparted to me by the priest with the palsied chin.

The chief priest, who until then had been mute, now spoke; out of his throat came a crooked falsetto. It was his duty, he said, to recite the evidences and conditions, the signs and confirmations, that had brought me to this hour of initiation. It was known that my mother had, despite all, been a woman of piety, dedicated to Hestia, before whose domestic shrine she had faithfully submitted her reverence; and that after her death, having denuded my house of all manner of precious things, as affirmed by the merchants of the agora, I retained and continued my mother's allegiance: the proof being the shrine itself, carried away by an acolyte enjoined to seek corroboration. Secondly, it was known that even from earliest childhood it was my passion to frequent the holy chapels in order to search out the veracity and power of their deities. Thirdly, it was attested by the kiln masters that as a young girl I was heard disputing with my father on behalf of the gods. And fourthly—

As if overcome by a chill, the chief priest halted.

Already there were intimations of the night to come, deepened by the long cold shadows of the stones. I looked into his face, that part of it visible above the great beard with its ornaments, and in the dwindling light saw an elderly man my own age, whose voice was strangely broken and stunted and shrill, akin to an infant's cry; and I knew him.

Fourthly, he resumed in that childlike pitch, your father's blood has become as water, and now you are freed and made holy. Dangerous and despised, an interloper and a blasphemer, he came among us only to usurp our native treasure. Him the gods have justly destroyed. Behold! I, Grand Priest and First Servant to the Oracle, hereby annul the stain!

The acolytes, meanwhile, had brought me to a flat stone close to the spring, where, encircled by a tall ring of concealing stones, I was made to prostrate myself. Over me stood the chief priest. He himself, he piped, was witness to the child I once was, and how in the cathedral shrine of Hestia, guardian of the civic hearth, and in the glimmer of the sacral flame between her thighs, he saw me overtaken by those signs of election given only to whom the goddess anoints: the sacerdotal frenzy, its telltale howls and whirlings, the shrieks of terror and elation at the instant of possession. It was by the will of the goddess that I should be as I now was: old and foretold, and virgin, and a woman apart.

As I lay there, smelling the damp earth, my face a brief space above the ground, I was aware of something alive and moist licking its way across the naked soles of my feet. It humped and curled as it slid into view: here was the habitation of snakes.

And so began what I was to become. To all these things—the admonitions and the testimonies, the rites and the annunciations—I had easily acquiesced. It was as well to live among stones as to linger emptily under the rotted lintel of my father's house. And if I wished, might I not readily escape this place—to go where? Too quickly I learned that my naked feet were my prison. When one bloody wound healed, another would open—either I blundered into a nest of thorns, or unwittingly cut my heel on a half-buried stone, sharp as an arrow. By cushioning leaves and grasses on a scrap of bark, and twining them round with the vines that crawled among the stones, I contrived to be roughly shod. The acolytes, I discovered, were indifferent to this and every other transgression. When I spoke to them, they answered freely; in the absence of the priests, they were no more than careless boys. I would hear them laughing and cavorting as they approached, and too often it happened that the meal they were carrying was spilled; and then I was left to go hungry.

It was from the acolytes that I came to know how our sibyl had met her death—not by divine command, as proclaimed by the priests, but by the bite of a snake in the heel. A commonplace: such a calamity might befall anyone, even in so mundane and frequented a spot as the agora itself. I had no fear of the snakes; they lived as I now lived, earthbound among the stones. I saw them as neighbors and companions, and at times amused myself by trailing them to their lairs; in this way I stumbled on a trove of sweet berries to gladden my hunger. Now and again, when one of these beasts lay motionless in a coil, in a fit of rapture I would be moved to study the colors and patterns of its skin, as I had once been stirred by the colors and patterns of my father's pots at the kilns. And all around, the stones in the changing light showed their changing tempers: the configurations of their small shadowed juttings and hollows came to resemble human features. More than once it seemed that my father's face looked out at me.

I had no desire to leave this place. It was sufficient. My feet, latterly growing callused and tough, were at last freeing me to wander away—yet why should I? If a piercing wind invaded, or if the sun blazed too harshly, the tall stones shielded me. I bathed when I pleased, I slept and woke when I pleased. The acolytes, like the days and the nights in their passing, came and went. The polis and its disorders were distant.

But I was in dread of the moon. I watched as it swelled, evening by evening; soon the priests would return. And at the time fixed for divination, when the moon was white and round and seamed with bluish veins, they arrived as they had before, in a procession, wordlessly. Behind them came the acolytes, carrying great waxed tablets—so many petitions and devotions, undertakings and devisings, ordinances and decrees, how they frightened me! All were to pass through me when the goddess entered my body.

I was made to wear a gown of pure linen—it girdled my neck and fell to my knees; my breasts it left bare. I was ashamed of my old woman's dried-up nipples and wrinkled dugs, but for these too I had been chosen: the proud gods disdain rivals to their beauty. No one envies a crone.

And my feet were again naked, but ugly and yellowed and hard as shells.

The chief priest drew me to the spring, where I was made to mount the flat stone of my initiation. Here I was to remain sequestered by the surrounding upright stones, and here I was to summon the goddess. Had I eaten or drunk that day? I said I had not. Though the acolytes had been instructed to withhold my meals, all afternoon I had glutted on berries and cupped my hands at the spring.

Then now you must drink.

He set down at my feet a silver kalyx and left me. I saw through the gaps in the stones how the priests with their tablets had gathered in a knot, silent and waiting; but I saw only their backs. It was forbidden to come near. It was forbidden to witness the act of possession.

I picked up the kalyx and looked into its mouth.

Swaying from side to side, as if agitated by some double tide, was a viscous purple sea. Its odor was foul. Its fumes were bitter.

And what must I do now?

I lifted my arms to the white moon and called to the goddess. Come. Come, I called, again and again. Come. Only come.

She did not come, and what must I do now?

The moonlight had carved small pits and grooves in the stones that hemmed me round like sentinels, and I saw my father's eyes, black and lidless, gaping out of the nearest stele; and I knew what I must not do.

I must not succumb. I must not surrender.

I stood erect on the sacral mound and from the lip of the kalyx slowly, slowly, spilled stain upon stain into the waters of the spring, observing how purple bled into red, and how red paled to clear transparency, until the spring flowed as innocently as before.

And then I gave out a great hideous shriek, and another, and another, my throat grappling more and more violently in its box, and I beat the stone at my feet, pounding and pounding with the silver kalyx, until a savage ringing raged all around, as if a phalanx of gongs were tumbling out of the night, and I spewed out unearthly words that were no words, only crippled syllables and feral growls and squeals, and I barked like a hound and hissed like a cat, and humped and crawled on my belly in the way of the snakes, and I clawed at my hair to twist it into worms, and thrashed and flailed on my slab, and writhed and cackled and yowled, and all the while I held on and held on, I would not succumb, I dared not surrender; and the goddess did not come.

She did not come, and I fell to the ground emptied, breathless; spent. No shaft of exaltation had penetrated the hollows of my body, I was what I was born to be, no more than mortal woman, and below all my clamor a brutal silence, the silence of the oracle that never was and never will be, the merciless silence of the goddess who never was and never will be, and now the voices of the priests, chanting, importuning, praising and blessing the goddess's terrifying power, her pity and absolution, crying out their tremulous petitions and grievances, their perplexities and yearnings, their ordinances and vainglorious decrees, all in submission to the sublime will—and what was I to do now, I who am deceiver and dissembler, false in ecstasy, false in frenzy, I who carry the blood of him who was not, and did not wish to be, one of us?

*

I have since outlived them all, the chief priest with his castrato mewlings, and the priest with the palsied chin, and I have outlived even the heedless acolytes, all of them given way to new priests and new careless boys. Always there will be the priests, and always there will be my companions the snakes with their unfeeling eyes and radiant skins, and always and always the tall stones that shelter my shrine. Nowadays I cover my feet with thick leather clogs (I have already been bitten twice, but mildly, and the fever soon passed), and when it is very cold, I make a fire if it pleases me (the acolytes bring the wood), and all in all I live as I like, and am content.

In the roundings of time, the acolytes seem always the same, the older reticent, the younger garrulous, and both uncommonly beautiful—the chief priests, I believe, choose them for their lovely mouths and soft napes. The younger is eager to give me news of the polis, how once in an unhappy autumn the remnants of my father's house were razed to rubble by a whirling storm, brief and already half-forgotten, which was said to cause scores of ships to be shattered, so that the traders no longer arrive, and the kiln masters are gone elsewhere to establish their craft anew. And in the fields beyond the agora, there are now wine presses and oil presses, bringing much prosperity. The charred grasses are again green, and the wildflowers dense, and throughout the polis order and serenity.

The priests go on, as of old, appealing to the goddess for holy guidance; but it is I who sanction and govern and make the laws, though the priests cannot know this. I no longer fear the growing moon and the wine with its treacheries, and the coming of the priests in procession cannot shake me. I am their mistress, and if I howl and convulse on the sacred mound, I do it not to indulge their belief, but to scorn it: the gods are a lie. Yet how accuse these solemn elders of delusion? As much accuse the snakes of their venom; it is their truth.

And I have learned, in time, to reveal the goddess's answer in the form of a puzzle, or a riddle, or an enigma with as many sides as a polygon: when diligently parsed, they cannot fail of reason or usefulness. As for the wine, always I am careful to paint the waters of the spring with its ebbing colors; but sometimes I leave a little at the bottom of the kalyx to give to the acolytes when they bring the morning meal. The older is reluctant and afraid, but the younger drinks lustily.

My father's image has faded from the nubs and crevices of the stones, and I scarcely ever look for it there. But on still summer nights, when ships are safe at sea, and the snakes hide in their thickets, and the spring runs soundlessly, and even the stones are tranquil, I think of that primitive and barbarous land, my father's home country, where their tongue is not our tongue, and their bread is not our bread, and their tales are not our tales, and they keep no sibyl and know no gods . . . then who is it that gives them their laws, lacking, as they do, one such as I?

Sin

By the last week of April, the parking lot's long chain-link fence already bristles with its hundreds of attachments: coiled wire, duct tape, butterfly clips, boat hooks, coat hangers, pellets of industrial glue, nylon strips, braided strings, and whatever other contraptions stubborn inge-nuity can dream up. Elsewhere, there are the uptown gal-leries, discreet and sleek as salons, with their Japanese pots on polished lion-pawed tables, and the walls behind them hung with small framed paintings ratified by catalogues signaling critical repute. And of course the grand muse-ums with their marble stairs and broken-nosed Roman busts in halls mobbed by foreign tourists.—Well, so what and hoity-toity and never mind! With us fence daubers, it's catch-as-catch-can, whoever happens to pass by, and it's smelly too, because of the pretzel man's salty cart on one end of our sidewalk and the soda man's syrupy cart on the other, and always the sickening exhaust from the cars grumbling every half hour in and out of the parking lot. And the hard rain, coming on without so much as a warning cloud to shut down business for the day, and all of us scrambling to cover our merchandise with plastic sheeting, which anyhow the wind catches up and tangles and carries away, along with someone's still life.

I call it merchandise. I don't presume to call it art, though some of it might be, and our customers, or clients, or loitering gawkers, or whatever they are, mostly wouldn't know the difference. As for us, we're all sorts— do-it-yourself souvenir peddlers (you can pay a dollar to coat a six-inch plaster Statue of Liberty in silver glitter), or middle-aged Bennington graduates in jeans torn at the knee who speak of having a "flair," or homeless fakes, soused and stinking and grubbing for coins, who put up pages cut from magazines, or part-time coffee-shop servers self-described as art students. With the exception of the sidewalk chalkers who sprawl on their bellies, indisputably sovereign over their squares of pavement, we are warily territorial. We are all mindful of which piece of fence belongs to whom, and which rusted old folding chair, and who claims the fancier plastic kind swiped from outdoor tables set out by restaurants in the good weather. And there are thieves among us too: if you don't keep an eye out, half your supplies will disappear, and maybe even your wallet.

I am one of those art students, though it's been a long while since I stood before an easel staring at a bowl of overripe pears while trying to imagine them as pure color and innate form. This was happening in the Brooklyn studio of my mentor at the time—*mentor* was his word for it, at a fee of seventy-five dollars per session. He had a habit of repeating a single, faintly sadistic turn of phrase: what I needed was discipline, he told me, and as my mentor he was naturally obliged (the meanly intended clever laugh came here) to be my *tor*mentor. I had an unhealthy tendency toward literalism, he explained, which it was his responsibility to correct. He regarded himself as a disciple of the legendary Philip Guston, but only in his early period. After three months or so, I couldn't bring myself to believe in the platonic souls of pears, and besides, my uncle Joseph in Ohio, who was subsidizing those pears even while under the impression that I was learning fashion illustration, was coming to visit the Avenue A walkup I shared with a Cooper Union engineering student and his girlfriend. Joseph had taken me on as a good deed after my stepfather died. He wasn't exactly my uncle; he was my stepfather's brother, and he was proposing, along with some necessary business in New York, to look me up to see how I was doing. I saw then that the flow of money was about to dry up—the money for my tormentor and the money for my half of the rent: the engineering student was soon to graduate and marry and start a job upstate. Within two days Joseph flew back to Cincinnati, betrayed.

"Goddam it, Eva, you're a goddam *orphan*," he threw back at me, "and look at you, cohabiting with a pair of degenerates, and those imbecile oozings piled up in that dump, you've played me for a fool—"

He hadn't believed me when I told him that the study of swirls and random swipes was a prerequisite for fashion design.

Joseph's sloughing me off left me nervous: fences can't supply steady cash the way uncles do. Still, I knew I wasn't meant for the garment industry. Only a year ago I had been blissfully in love with the Pre-Raphaelites.

I began to wait tables from seven to midnight at La Bellamonte, an Italian restaurant down the street from the fence. And it was I who carried off two plastic sidewalk chairs, one for the portraitist (this was what we called ourselves), and one for the sitter. It was good to be literal—to work up a reasonable likeness—though not too much. For portraits, a bit of prettying was always preferable. Beginning about May, when the weather warmed up, straight through the middle of October, the money was reliable. I would charge according to how my sitter was dressed, though I was often wrong. I was amazed by the vanity of what I took to be, from the condition of their shoes, the poor: they were willing to pay as much as five dollars without giving me an argument, and sometimes I just tore the sheet off the pad and handed it over for free. Of course I sold what I could of the stuff I hung on the fence: these I splashed out quickly, between sitters—fanciful birds on branches, Greek-shaped vases overflowing with flowers (I had a botany book to copy from), invented landscapes, some with mountains, some with lakes. If there were lakes, I sketched in a boat with French lovers in old-fashioned headgear, huge feathered brims for the women and top hats for the men. From the local pharmacy, one of those acres-wide brilliantly lit warehouses where you could find anything from cheese crackers to lampshades, I bought cheap wood frames and painted them white. This gave the pictures on my three yards of fence almost a look of settled elegance.

Weekends, Sundays especially, are our busiest time, when people stroll by with their sodas or dripping popsicles (there's an ice cream vendor one block over) to watch the portraitists at work. For onlookers like ours, a portrait is an event requiring the courage to decide which of us to choose, and a certain daring even to submit to a twenty-minute sitting, surrounded by all the public kibbitzers who comment on the process, whether this person's nose is really wider than it's been shown, or taking note of a wattle that's been brushed away. Generally the crowd works itself up into a mood of untamed but not unfriendly hilarity. Yet sometimes it will be cruel.

It was cruel to the woman in the blue suit. She was not unfamiliar. I had spotted her yet again when, on the third Sunday in a row, she turned up, gaping with all the others circling round my easel. The weather was unusually hot for a late August afternoon coming on toward evening, and the baking pavement, with its crackle of pretzel crumbs, was still burning the feet of the pigeons; they were hopping more than pecking. Or else they were sated. As for me, I'd already counted one hundred and fifty-two dollars, more than enough for a single day's work, and was beginning to pack up the little it was my habit to take away for the night—brushes, paints, botany book, easel (the folding kind). The paintings I would leave where they were. I threw a worn tarp (pilfered from a car in the lot) over my part of the fence and with a piece of narrow rope knotted it through the gaps in the steel. What if rowdies came and ran off with my landscapes and flowers and boats? I would deem it a compliment, and anyhow I could readily splash out a few more.

By now many of the gawkers had dispersed, and the pretzel and soda men were long gone. But the diehards were still milling on the sidewalk, with bottles in paper bags bulging from hips and armpits. The woman in the blue suit was among them, cautious, attentive. Watchful.

As I was maneuvering the easel into its carrier, she called out, "Not yet, not yet!"

"Sorry," I said, "I'm just leaving, I can't be late."

"Why should I care, I'll take my turn now. I don't like it with that riffraff all around. So now."

"Sorry," I said again. "I've seen you before, haven't I? Then maybe next time? Or instead"—I lifted an edge of the tarp—"you could take home one of these, I'd let you have this one for half the price. A scene on the water." It was the feathered brim and the top hat.

"I don't want that kitsch. I want you at the easel. I want to see up close how you do it. I know what I want." This hint of disputation drew the diehards. Some of them already had the mouths of the bottles in their mouths. "All you people, get out of my way. Scum!"

Here was authority. And authority was money. The austere blue suit, of some summery fabric I couldn't name, the lapis necklace, the crucial absence of earrings, the gold loops on her wrists, and especially the tiny laced shoes, of that blue called midnight. Oddly small feet, a tidy head on a thin neck—she was small all over. Voice an uncontained ferocity. She looked to be—she could easily have been— a regular at the uptown galleries. And with her surliness she had mocked the surliest remnant of the crowd.

They mocked back. They called her cross-eyed (this she was, very slightly), they laughed at her skinny neck and her little feet, they laughed at me for surrendering to her whim. Once again I set up the easel. She took her place on one of the plastic chairs with an angry stubbornness that soon became a barrier. My own chair I had shoved aside; if I stood, I might dominate. Her face, I thought, had traces of insult, the eyelids tightened at the outer corners. How old was this woman? A portraitist, even my sort of sidewalk quick-job, relies on age; it animates character. But her fixed stare, guiding the brush and judging its pacings, gave out nothing. I bent closer to see the color of her irises. In the lessening light they had a yellow tint.

"Stop ogling," she spat out, "just get on with it, I'm not sitting here all night—"

The sun was dropping behind the parking lot. The last of the hecklers, finally bored, dwindled and scattered. I hurried to finish, forsaking detail, drizzling a mist of hair of indeterminate tone (was it brown, was it gray?), and privately calculated my price. The woman in the blue suit was rich; she had money. Rich people have good clothes, nice shoes, fine teeth. My uncle Joseph had paid thousands for his implants. On the other hand, this woman had sought out a street painter at a parking lot fence, so perhaps she was no different from the forlorn in their rotted sandals . . . yet how could this be? Her insistence had the brittle scrape of worldliness. She was a force. I lifted the sheet from the easel and held it out to her.

"Look at that thing, what would I want with that? It's the hand I'm after, I told you, seeing it up close, the grip, that little bit of hesitation just after—"

She snatched up her likeness—I'd caught her well enough, that angry lower lip, those inharmonious eyes— and tore it in two.

I said, "You have to pay anyway, I've done the work, you have to pay."

She drew from a flap of the blue suit a tiny blue purse. "Here, take this"—it was four one-hundred-dollar bills—"and there could be more. Does Sol Kerchek mean anything nowadays? I didn't think it would, you're too young."

I contemplated the name: nothing. I contemplated her money. It was still in her grasp.

"He's ancient history, people don't remember. I had someone all picked out last month, a boy, I found him crouched in a corner so the guard wouldn't see. He was copying a Klimt. But in the end he was no good. He had the hand, but the whole thing was over his head. So," she said, "are you taking these or not?"

She wiggled the four bills under my chin. The engineer and his girlfriend, I knew, were already packing their belongings. In a few days they'd be gone, and my rent would instantly double.

"In the beginning," she pushed on, "you'd only have to clean brushes and so on, keep the place from getting overrun with rags. After that it's all up to him, whatever he wants."

"I've got a job, I don't have time for another—"

But already I saw that La Bellamonte would not soon claim me again.

She gave me that askew look; there was triumph in it.

"You don't have time for Sol Kerchek? You don't have time for a man whose work sits in Prague, in Berlin, in Cracow? In London? Those were the old days, but he's not dead yet, he's worth something. You should get on your knees for the privilege, you don't deserve what I'm offering—"

I shot back: "You ripped up my work, you called my stuff kitsch!"

"I say what I say and I see what I see." She stuffed the bills into the pocket of my shirt. "Come on, it's only a ten-minute walk from here."

I followed her then, threading through the gathering evening crowds on the sidewalks, past the red and green neon blinks of bars and suspect dance halls, past news-stands hung with key chains and caps and sunglasses, past check-cashing storefronts, bauble vendors, boys handing out flyers for fortune-tellers. The air was seeded with the fumes of lemony hookahs, and from the open doors of a row of ill-lit cafés, many with insolent old awnings, came the whine of guitars and a scattered pattern of clapping. We were coming now into darkened streets lined with tall silent after-hours glass-coated office buildings. A few windows were randomly lit.

"This is his place," the woman in the blue suit said. Between a pair of these giant vitrines stood a small clap-board house with a high stoop. Part of the siding was covered with stucco; the stucco showed meandering cracks, barely visible in the glow of the streetlamp. Crushed by the brutes on either flank, the little house seemed to quiver with its own insufficiency.

"We put in a skylight a few years ago, but with the way his eyes are now there's no point, all that construction debris and birdshit and whatnot, even the sun can't push through. And these monoliths they put up, there's no light anyhow. They tried to bribe us to sell, that's how they do it, but he wouldn't give in, it's like that with the old. Well look, here's something convenient."

I saw a concrete city trash bin.

She grabbed my easel—I had been carrying it tilted over my shoulder, like a rifle—and tossed it in. The plastic carrier tore with a screech.

"You won't need that anymore. There's a better one upstairs."

I trailed her up the eight steps of the stoop, denuded.

"It's these steps," she said. "He never goes out. And then the staircase going up, it's too much."

In the vestibule, an abrupt patter of foreign voices. The smell of something frying. Sol, she told me, had the apartment at the top. The whole place, from end to end, was his studio. The people on the lower floor were a Filipino couple, the man ailing; only the woman mattered, she brought Sol his dinner every night, she cleaned his awful toilet, she changed his sheets. I wouldn't have to do anything like that, she assured me. Maybe now and then I could boil water for his tea, find him a cracker to go with it. My responsibility was solely to his art, did I understand?

I asked about the hours and the money.

"The hours are whatever he says, whatever he wants. And let me worry about the money."

She showed me what I took to be a business card and then pinched it away. I had only a moment to see MARA KERCHEK, CONSULTANT, and a row of digits below.

"He won't have a phone, he doesn't like to be bothered, he says he can't hear. If you think you might want me, you can text me."

"I can't," I admitted. "Someone swiped my phone. Nothing's safe at that fence—"

"Oh fine, incommunicado, the blind leading the blind. Go get yourself a new one." It was a command. "Not that you'll ever want me up there."

Mara Kerchek. So the old man must be her father. His door, a heavy thing with carved scrolls, was half open. A relic purloined from some nobler house.

"Sol!" she called. "I've got someone."

I had expected him to be small, like Mara Kerchek. He was stooped, with the bony spikes of massive shoulders leading down to a pair of uncommonly large and dirty hands. Every fingernail carried its load of dried paint, mostly blackened. A wayward white thicket smothered his big head, and around it a hint, even a halo, of hugeness, like a ghost of the mountain he must once have been. The fuzz on his slippers was trembling.

"Mara, Mara!" With tentative balance he tipped forward to embrace her, and I saw that his eyes, droop-lidded and milky-pale and full of sleep, were emphatically unlike hers. She let him hold out those monstrous hands long enough for a single heave of his breath—ponderous, sluggish—and then patted them away. Or was it a mild slap?

"My little Mara," he said. "All in blue, all in blue, look how beautifully she dresses, she's always dressed that way, she knows how to do it, she always knew, even at the start—"

But she cut him off. "He likes to talk a lot, don't you, Sol? You don't have to listen," she told me. "And he won't use his cane. The way he moves, make sure he uses his cane."

The little blue shoes quick-tapped down the stairs.

"She indulges me, you saw that." He was looking me

over with, I felt, a dubious fastidiousness. "Last time it was that boy, couldn't tell his left from his right. But she means to please me, she has a merciful heart."

"She was in a hurry to get away," I said.

"She has her work."

Under the muddy skylight (it was night now) I took in a scene of stasis. Stillness and disuse. A tall thick-legged tripod, naked and faceless as a skeleton, and near it a low table littered with dozens of dried-out paint pots and a jar of hideous brushes, heavy and stiffened. A four-footed cane hooked over a battered wooden chair. The dusky room itself as long and narrow as some corridor in a gloomy hotel. At the far end I made out a pair of dirty windows—dirty even in the dark. And when I switched on the only lamps I could discover—all three had torn silk shades—the cluttered walls on either side of Kerchek's studio (it was Mara Kerchek who had named it that) bluntly revealed what I had caught sight of but hadn't accounted for. Those lumpy silhouettes were canvases, masses of canvases stacked back to back, wild and unframed, flaming, stricken with a crisis of color, the paint as dense as if sculpted.

And between the walls, a chaise longue, tattered only a little, dangling crimson tassels over curly squat feet, islanded in the void under the blinded skylight. All around, a public smell—the smell of Kerchek's toilet. It drifted from space to space, mingling, I imagined, with

the fetid odors of worn and crippling age. It was clear that
the woman in the apartment below was negligent; the
care of the toilet, and the abhorrent hollow of the grubby
cubicle that was Kerchek's kitchen, and the jungly bed I
glimpsed in the dim hollow behind it, would fall to me,
and what was I, why was I here? If sometimes the woman
below failed to turn up with his meal, would I be obliged
to forage in some nearby midnight diner for whatever
might pass for Sol Kerchek's supper?

I got rid of the decaying brushes and filled the jar
with my own. I made some small order in the sticky
kitchen. I gathered up armfuls of paint-soaked oily rags
furry with dust—the accumulation of years—and tossed
them into the city's trash bin; my easel was gone. From
under Kerchek's bed I pulled out a roll of canvas grayed by
grime, and a torn cardboard box heaped with stale tubes
of oils. I twisted one open; out sputtered a clot of brilliant
turquoise.

And all the while the four-footed cane still hung dis-
obediently from the wooden chair. Mara Kerchek had
snapped out an order; Kerchek refused it. Then why
shouldn't I defy Mara Kerchek, why must I satisfy Mara
Kerchek? What would I do with a phone in this timeless
feral place, where an old man's breathings were measured
only by a faraway sun moving languidly across an opaque
skylight? Here was freedom, and leisure, and unexpected ease. My wages, delivered by the woman below,

sometimes came, and sometimes did not, and always in the shape of one-hundred-dollar bills sealed in an envelope coiled in masses of tape, its thickness impossible to predict. One envelope might be skimpy, the next one fat. I was content; ever since my uncle Joseph had given up on me, I had never felt so flush. Mara Kerchek herself kept away.

In the afternoons, it was Kerchek's habit to totter, caneless, toward that grotesquely ornamental object under the skylight, where he dropped into a doze. He lay there among its royal cushions like some misshapen odalisque, dozing and waking, dozing and waking, and soon enough he would shudder, hotly aware, into an excited cry, a remnant of some dream. His dreams, he told me, were omens and alarms—catastrophic, shaming. And more than once he explained how this misplaced Oriental curiosity came to flutter its fringes between the walls.

"My paradise, my sanctum," he said. "Look how my Mara indulges me. She found this marvel, who knows where she picked it up, she finds me everything, she found me that door, she found me that boy who didn't know his left hand from his right hand, she found me you, and do you know why? My foolish little Mara believes in instinct. She believes in resurrection. It's all mumbo jumbo. Superstition."

His voice puzzled me. Ingratiating, taunting, as if it concealed a fear.

In those early weeks, in the empty hours when Kerchek clung to his divan, and at other times too, I might easily have wandered off into the city streets on musings of my own, or walked the halls of the great museums uptown, where the world's imagination was stored. Instead, I searched out a pastry shop tucked among those glassed-in office buildings, and went every day to buy muffins and little cakes and canisters of foreign teas and blocks of oddly colored cheeses to fill Kerchek's blighted cupboard. And once, in a half-hidden alley, I blundered into a lively bodega, and returned with eggs and onions and potatoes and sometimes a bit of fish. In the evening, if the woman below brought up a soup that was too thin, or dry chicken parts more bone than flesh, I would cook up a stew or fry an egg. He was indifferent to my comings and goings. It was enough that I was there, to sit with him over teacups, mutely listening as he recited his sorrowful dreams, or spooled out what he called his misgivings, his guilts, his remorse.

"In those days," he always began, and then he would speak of the time before the war, and what war was that? All those wars, how was I to know, was it a war before I was born, or after? Why was I here, what was I meant to do?

The skylight was turning autumnal.

"Eva." He rasped this out with a lordliness that surprised me. After so many muffins and little pink cakes and cups of tea—after so many rueful mutterings—it was the first time he had spoken my name. Then he asked how old I was.

"I can't tell from your face. My eye can't see eyes. Faces gone, color no, my Mara in blue—" All this staccato, like gunshot.

I told him I was twenty-three. But I put my head down. To admit to this meagerness was a humiliation. Mara Kerchek had already parsed it: how could I deserve to be in this place with an old man's spiraling regrets, when I had none at all?

"Well, so much for that. My little Mara was twenty-six when we started, and how ambitious she was! And how cleverly she dressed even then, the way she carried herself, it gave her entry, you know, to the galleries, they saw her belief, they took on her belief—"

He stopped to attend to one of his slowly toiling breaths. I watched his torso, bent as it was, climb and recede, climb and recede.

"She hawked my work. After a while they came to her from everywhere. She made us rich. Never mind that she exaggerates, she lies a little, she indulges me, she makes you think Louvre, she makes you think Prado, it was nothing like that, but in those days," and he returned again to the time before the war, when his paintings were coveted, when his name was coveted, when there was everything all at once, everything newborn, a gluttony for the never before, schools and movements and trends and solemn revolutions, the orphists, the purists, the futurists, the vorticists, and soon the action painters, he was with it all, in the swim, in the maelstrom of all that delirium, and it was easy for Mara to make them rich. Especially during his divanist period (it was Mara who thought of calling it that), his conceptual nudes, his minimalist nudes, his spatter nudes, all of them parting their legs on sprawling velvet couches.

And sometimes, he told me, it was Mara who posed naked for him on that cheap chaise longue they'd bought, in those days, right out of the Sears, Roebuck catalogue.

I asked if Mara would come, if he expected her to come.

"She keeps away," I said.

"She has her work. It wears her out."

He stared me down with his milky eyes. Untamed wads of hair spilled over his collarbones. And again that stale aurora of things long eclipsed, those old grievances, if that's what they were, unfurling hour after hour, the same, the same. And then again the same. The spittle on his lip when he scraped out yet another weighty breath. He looked, I thought, like someone's abandoned messiah.

"My Mara is estranged," he said. "I've disappointed her, I haven't been good to her. She made us rich, I made her poor. After the war I made her poor."

Poor? The lapis pendant, the gold bracelets, the

perfected blue shoes with their satin laces, the silken blue suit (was it silk, was it something else), the hundred-dollar bills?

I asked him if he would allow me to trim his hair.

His mind was all Mara. *Mara, Mara, my little Mara.* And wasn't I his echo? *Daughter, father,* banished words, useless here. Only Mara, Mara.

"She has a merciful heart," he said, "she indulges me, but still she casts me out, she doesn't relent. Year after year, after the war."

He told me where I might find a scissors—under the dirty windows, at the far end of his studio, beyond the skylight, in the deep drawers of a tall corner cabinet. The scissors were there, and a hammer and a vial of small black nails, and a roll of new canvas, and a sack of fresh tubes of oils. And a crisscross of stretcher bars. Mara, he explained, had ordered that boy to bring in all these useless things, that boy who didn't know his left hand from his right hand, and what good was any of it anyhow?

"The eye is the hand," he said. "And without the eye, the hand is as good as dead."

Shards of hair flew to the floor. I bent over him to do away with the tangled woolly forelock, and then his head was close against me, and I could feel in my ribs the heat of his history as he wove and unwove the knit of what was, how with all his generation of men (but he was older than most) he had been made to go to that faraway war, first in a massive ship, and then the landing on a blasphemous continent, its cities of slaughter, its trenches and shootings, planes like fleas in the sky, men who were wolves to men, women who covered their breasts with their hands, human flesh smoldering, and he saw and he saw and he saw, and he knew and he knew and he knew, and what he knew was that the body of the earth is cut in two by a ditch. A ditch between two walls.

But I had worked too close to the scalp. There was little left to cover the violated head. It was as if I had excavated a skull.

"In those days," he went on, "when the war was finished, when the war had evaporated, everything swept back to before, again the new, the new," and he told of the new office buildings, the new neighborhoods, the new hem lengths, the new markets, the galleries hungry for buyers, the collectors hungry for prestige, the contractors hungry to dazzle their suites, and oh how Mara believed! She assured him that he had only to resume. He was older than most, he was weary, he'd come out alive from the precincts of sin, and why, he asked, must he resume? She knew exactly, she was impatient to begin, she was inspired, the newest thing wasn't the newest thing, the newest thing was the oldest thing, she had been gazing, gazing, walking the Guggenheim, walking MoMA, in library reading rooms paging through catechisms of paintings, their periods, their masters, they fed her instincts, she had the clairvoyance of her instincts, and she hummed out the names of the old divanists, the old luxuriant gods, Modigliani, Matisse, Delacroix, Morisot, even Millet, even Boldini, divanists all, and more and more! She was in the thick of things, she was in the know, she could scent what the market craved, what it ought to crave, what she would teach it to crave, what the collectors devoured.

It was naked women lying down.

"She wanted me to go back to the divans. She wanted me to remake them in the shapes of all the new crazes, dance to the new tunes, old profits in new clothes, all her contacts were waiting, all her old clients, all those rich men looking for the latest thing. Retrofit, assemble, usurp, they could call it any fool name they liked, it was divans, divans, and what else was it but my Mara undressed and lying down? Still," he said, "look around, look around, and tell me if I haven't repented—"

He drilled a thick finger with its thickened fingernail through the darkening air, as if it could span the ditch between the walls, where, on either side, those heaps of canvases leaned moribund in the dust. The woman below came with his evening meal. The soup was again thin. He spooned it up and sent the rest away. Already, for many days, he had spurned the cheeses, the muffins, the little pink cakes; but he went on warming his hands on his tea-cup. I no longer sought out the pastry shop; it sickened him. The bodega, hidden in its alley, had anyhow failed. He took to using his cane.

In late November a peculiar brightness fell. Overhead, soundless cushions folding and unfolding: it had snowed in the night. The burdened skylight, soaked in sun, poured down rivers of white. The light, the light!

I asked if I might turn the canvases to the light.

"She couldn't move a single one," he said. "Not a one. The bleedings of three years, when I still had the eye, when I still had the hand. She begged for the divans. Instead I gave her these. Go turn them if you want, but I warn you, I warn you—"

I saw how heavily he lowered his big shoulder bones and the warp of his spine into the wooden chair where the cane had been shunned; but now he cherished it. And in an instant of shame I regretted cutting his hair. There was nothing to conceal his meaning. His meaning was transgression. He sat like a witness. It was, I felt, a vigil. Or a rite. A judgment. The vacant tripod stood nearby.

In that unnatural snowy light—or because of it, because it illumined the shadowy walls with unaccustomed clarity—I was at liberty to turn and turn each canvas, to see into this one, to inhabit that one, even to be repelled by all of them. To be warned and judged and sentenced. I saw how they were afflicted by a largeness. Even the smallest conveyed a looming. I saw what I imagined to be scenes, a ferryboat overturned, fires ingesting whole towns, drownings, earthquakes, scorching lava—but almost immediately I knew these to be illusions, the tricks of color and form and the impulsive licks of the brush. The tricks of largeness, of appetite for ruin. I thought of the scored palms of Kerchek's elephantine hands.

I crossed from wall to wall. Between these frenzies a ditch. Smoke, seared flesh, anguish, trains, engines, silent explosions. Yet hadn't he warned me? I was not to do what that ignorant boy had done, the boy who didn't know his left hand from his right hand. I was not to mistake a canvas on the left wall for a canvas on the right wall. I was not to misplace, I was not to compare. They were distinct, one wall from the other. And mutually alien: each an enemy to its opposite. Each wall was an archive. Each wall was a clamor. Each wall was a shriek. Right wall was at war with left wall.

These, he told me, were his repudiations, his repentance. In those days, when he still had his eye and his hand, they had the power to redeem. And now they festered.

"Mara couldn't place any of them," he said. "They weren't wanted. She didn't understand any of it, she didn't expect anyone to understand, she wanted the divans, she wanted the profits, they were there for the plucking, the postwar markets all on fire, why was I scheming to make her poor, was it vengeance?"

The sun had passed over the skylight. Kerchek's

studio—how forlorn it was—returned to its daytime dusk. The canvases were again what they had been: dead things decaying. In a hidden corner of each of them, an obscure sign: *SK*, intertwined like an ampersand.

I confessed that I could see no breach between one wall and the other. The wall on the right seemed no different from the wall on the left.

"You don't see, you don't see? You with your eyes, you can't see? It was Mara, my Mara, who made me see—"

I waited while he searched for his breath; I had learned to wait. A little snake of a laugh crept out of his throat. It frightened me; it meant he was waning. His afternoon dozes had grown longer and longer. I had cut his hair too close to the scalp, his head was naked, and what if he died before Mara came, what was I to do? And when would she come?

It was Mara herself, the joke of it, he told me, who drove him on, who drove him into the work of the walls, if not for Mara he might have succumbed to the divans, scores of divans, hundreds of divans, seduced by the schools, the movements, the profits, the old made new. If not for Mara, after the war. She came to him, straight out, or how would he know to tell it now? An inchling, she called it, she did away with it, what else could she do, it was only an inchling, a pinch of fat in the womb, so why did it matter?

His poor little ambitious Mara, hoping to lure her

clients, her collectors, to please, to appease. Even then, even then.

And that discarded pinch of fat in the womb, was it the same as the poisonous brown seed of the apple, and if you crush the seed, you give the lie to the tree? Was it the same as the capsized ferry and its drownings? Was it the same as the bridge that collapses from age? Or the floods when the tide comes in, or the fires the winds ignite? Is the inferno in the belly of the earth the same as sin? Or the fever that kills? Is the river that dries no different from will? Who dares to fuse the two? Only a pinch of fat in the womb, so why must it matter?

"But I wept, you know," he said. "I wept. And then, because nothing mattered, not even a pinch of fat in the womb, I began to see again. I saw with all the strength of my body. Sin on one side, calamity on the other, with a ditch to keep them apart. Only men sin. Only women. It's an innocent God who wakens ruin."

I can't say that these were Kerchek's words. I can only say that this is what I heard. After all, he never spoke of God. He never mentioned sin, and hadn't he sneered at superstition? In fact, I remember that he said very little, only that once, long ago, while up to his knees in running blood on that blasphemous continent, Mara Kerchek conceived a child and did away with it.

And afterward—after letting out this small note—he went on dabbling his spoon in his soup.

The next day all that was forgotten. He warmed his hands on his morning tea and asked me plainly if I knew why Mara Kerchek had brought me to him.

"To be your assistant," I said. What else should I say?

"Did she do her hocus-pocus? Put you up for trial? My silly Mara with her sixth sense—"

"She called my work kitsch. She tore it up."

"Eva," he said, "come here. Give me your hand."

It startled me to hear him speak my name yet again; it seemed almost conspiratorial. I placed my left hand on his right hand. It lay there like a small salamander nestled among the mounds of his knuckles.

"Hocus-pocus," he said. "Abracadabra. She means to make it all come back to life. And do you know why?"

I had no answer. I feared his confidings, I feared his trust. If he was dying—the skin of his head was pitted and rusted and crumpled—if he was beginning to die, it wasn't for me to give him deliverance. He had a daughter for that!

"My Mara is sick of her work, it wears her out, I haven't been good to her. I've brought her down, I've made her poor—"

It was his usual chant. I thought I would tear through it outright.

I said, "Mara's work, what is it?"

"The same. Always the same. The clients, the consultations, the appraisals. These collectors, they want to possess but they don't know what they want to possess. She takes them around and shows them. Or else she goes up to their palaces, their penthouses, whatever they call them, to appraise what they already possess. The richer they are, the more they want to spell out the worth of things. The price. They're cautious, you know, so they pay in raw cash—"

Where was his breath? He was panting a little, a shallow gasp, and then another. A bit of a noise to go with it, and while I waited for the noise to subside, and for his breath to return, it came to me—how open it was—that Mara Kerchek in her silky blue suit, with her lapis necklace and satin shoeties, was a woman of the night.

In early December the day gave way to dark in seconds. The lamps were switched on before three, and Kerchek slept on, hour after hour, through the afternoon gloom. His feet, with their slippers fallen, overflowed the divan; the toenails tall and thick and jagged. The head on the ornate cushion a pallid dome. The soft ears uncovered. A remnant of biscuit left uneaten.

From the cabinet under the far windows I retrieved the scissors, the hammer, the vial of tacks. Out of the web of stretcher bars I chose four. I cut a length of fresh canvas, and hammered the bars into a precise fir square. I drew the canvas as taut as could be and tapped it down until it resisted the lightest dent of a fingertip. Then I snipped off the last wavering threads.

Through all this commotion I was vigilant. I kept watch over Kerchek's breast: was it rising and descending, was this wasted old man breathing? Was he deaf to the hammering? But he slept on. The pale canvas in its frame, resting now on the lip of the tripod, had the look of the white of an eye awaiting its pupil.

And meanwhile in these short December days that rush into night, the skylight turns biblical. Snow falls again, and then again, the wintry wind arouses the sun: let there be light! But the light is theatrical and brief, and must be made much of while it lasts.

It was in just such a snowstruck radiant interval, when Kerchek refused his dry biscuit and took up his cane and shed his slippers and let himself warily down into those velvety cushions to revisit his dreams (but the itch to reveal them had lately weakened), that I began to paint the divan. The divan overflowing with Kerchek.

I painted him slyly, slowly, thickly, hugely, with a raptness new to my hand. I painted his collarbones, the bare ruined pallor of his heels. I painted, with pity, his hands. I painted his looted head, the flattened mouth, the wrinkled ovals of his shuttered eyes. The ways of the fence, speed and slapdash, all for the money, were wicked here.

And I painted the divan, the velvet, the crimson, the cushions, the curly squat legs, the kingly tassels. For ten days I painted until it was too dark to see. I emptied the tubes of their greens and reds and yellows and taupes, and thickened and thinned them to grow into skin and weave and the gray of veins and the delusions of sleep: a vessel for Kerchek's mind. I knew what was in it. Dread and pity for such a daughter. Intoxicated by such a daughter.

The woman below stopped coming. It was pointless, he turned away. How I regretted cutting his hair, unclean, even savage. I had meant it for his dignity. Instead it left the bones of his face jutting. I painted them as if they were the crumbling bones of a pharaoh. And it was with something like reverence that I painted the divan: its sultan's cushions, its swaying tassels, its regally curlicued feet. Soon he would die there, I thought, on Mara Kerchek's divan.

The skylight's snow ebbed, the sun hid itself. The light was gone. A wind sent in the cold. The skin of Kerchek's hands, how like a membrane of thinnest isinglass, and under it the wormy dying veins. I covered his shoulders and arms with a blanket. He had no one to warm him. Mara kept away.

It was enough. Why was I here? The thing was finished.

"I'm going now, I have to go," I said, and looked down on him. "Mara will come," I told him. "Any day now she'll come."

He didn't wake. He didn't hear. I left him and went back to see what I had made. The figure on the divan, was it Kerchek? The resemblance was poor, who would know him? A heap of wornout passion. An unforgiven seer. The traitor father of a traitor daughter.

But the thing was done. Or almost. I picked up the brush with the slenderest tip and in a hidden fold of the canvas painted a tiny emblem: *SK*. It looked like an ampersand.

"Eva," he called. A voice hollowed by a stranded dream. "Eva, come here, I'm cold—"

His milky eyes were on guard. He took my hand, but this time he held me by the wrist and passed his heavy fingers over the palm. I felt how coarse they were.

"Do you have a mother? A father?"

"A stepfather, but he died."

"A child's hand. Small, like Mara's. She sees things in the fold of a thumb, in the turn of a crease." His fingers hardened on mine, one by one. "Mumbo jumbo, my Mara sees, she sees what she wants to see—"

It fell out like a plea.

"No," I said. "It's her father who sees."

"Mara? Mara's father is dead."

Was he a man condemning himself? Was it a sentence? A punishment? For the sin of making Mara poor.

"No, no, your daughter has a merciful heart, you say this yourself, she's bound to come soon—"

"My daughter? I have no daughter."

Was he grieving, was he lost? Or was it shame?

"You have Mara," I said.

I saw him let down his legs. I saw him pull himself up from the divan. The crimson tassels swung. His old man's head shook.

"What are you saying? I have no child, I have no daughter."

I said again, "You have Mara."

"Mara, Mara." His throat thickened. His eyes blackened into char. He threw off his grip on my wrist. "Is that what you think? Is that what you believe? Who told you such blasphemy? That I am the man who would uncover his own daughter's nakedness, that I am the father who would stretch out his daughter on a couch only to gaze on her lineaments? That I would oblige her to raise her hip for the curl of its arch, that I would beg her to part her thighs, and all for the sake of painter's gold? Ignorant girl, you don't know your left hand from your right hand, Mara is my wife, my little Mara, my wife, my wife—"

I can't say that these were Kerchek's words. I can only say that this was what I heard.

He sank back into the cushions. I saw his breast climb and recede, climb and recede.

"I have to go now," I said. "I can't stay," and left him there. Someone would find him. The woman below would find him. Or Mara would come.

★

Well, I'm back at La Bellamonte. Guido, the manager, gives me a second chance, he says, on condition that I never again walk out on the job. As penalty, he's taken five dollars off my old wages. What with the rent on my place, I can barely afford a new phone. Anyhow I've bought one. Who nowadays can live without such a thing? I've got a new shirt, too, with a zippered pocket to keep it safe. As for the rent, I was lucky enough to scout out a pair of art students from Cooper Union, to pay for half—Richard and Robert. They're focused and ambitious. Richard is heading for theater design, Robert for advertising. Like the engineer and his girlfriend, they sleep in one bed, mouth to mouth.

When the weather warms up, I'll go back to the fence. I won't do landscapes or seascapes or period lovers or flowers in vases or any of that sort of kitsch. I won't put anything up on the fence. I'll have a little table, the folding kind, and I'll filch a couple of chairs when Guido isn't looking, and what I'll do is miniatures. On fingernails, female and male. The women generally like ladies in long gowns. The men want snakes and daggers and girls' names circled in roses, the things you see tattooed on their biceps. All that, I'm told, is the newest craze down there at the fence, and brings in the money.

The Coast of New Zealand

To burn always with this hard, gemlike flame,
to maintain this ecstasy, is success in life.

—Walter Pater

The last time George and the three women met, it was on a warm October afternoon in that same small Greek restaurant, with bluish fluorescent lights overhead, in Stamford, Connecticut. Their knees were crowded under the tablecloth, and inadvertently rubbed one against another. Though they all wore glasses (Ruby was seriously myopic), even so it was difficult to read the menu.

"Nice," George said. "Gives the place the feel of a modest bordello." And only Evangeline laughed; Olive made a face, and Ruby sighed in disgust, but it was merely to tease. Not that it escaped him that behind the ribbing was an old and avid jealousy; they adored what they could not attain. He had decided on Stamford as the geographical midpoint of their reunion, he told them, because it was equidistant from wherever their fates might eventually drive them. It was the very center of the planet's fragile equilibrium. But why, they asked, this unprepossessing eatery smelling of fried eggplant? Because, he said, the eggplant is earth's most beautifully sculptured fruit.

The four of them had been at library school together, and had exchanged clandestine notes in a course on the history of books, which George, one of three males in the class, had named Spinsters 101. The two others he called Mouse One and Mouse Two. The notes were all about George, and George wrote notes about himself: *six feet two, brainy, unusual.* Or else: *early balding, doomed to success.* And once, nastily: *Lady librarians never marry.*

By the time they graduated, he had slept with all of them.

They had long ago forgiven him, and also one another. And they had all agreed to abide by the Pact—George's invention. Its terms were simple enough: once a year they were to gather at this very spot, if possible at their usual table (but they must insist on this), the one closest to the kitchen. All correspondence, any exchange of any kind in the long intervals between meetings, was forbidden. Tales of dailiness and its intimacies, their cluttered lives, their tiny news and parochial views were never to be the object of their coming together. Consensus was forbidden; the Pact was a treaty of solitary will. "Our interest," he explained, "lies in extremes. Abhor the mundane, shun the pedestrian. Cause the natural to become unnatural." And then this: "What is our object? To live in the whirlpool of the extraordinary. To aspire to the ultimate stage of fanaticism. To know that eventuality is always inevitability, that the implausible is the true authenticity." He spoke these words with the portentousness of Laurence Olivier as Henry V rallying the troops on St. Crispin's Day.

They were sensible women, and took it as the joke they believed it was meant to be: to live life as a witticism. As a feat. As an opera. But it was also an Idea, and George was a master of ideas. They had their Idea too: they were committed feminists, despised patriarchy, and loathed what they could instantly sense was male domination. George was exempted from such despicable categories. He was a schemer of witchcraft. His brain was neither male nor female. It was, they understood, a vessel of daring, and they had only to climb aboard to feel its oceanic sweep. They were not four, or three, or two. They were, counting George, One.

He had been drawn to them, lured by those dusty old curios—their preposterous names. It was as if they had been situated together the way artifacts similar in the taste of an era are collected in the same museum vitrine. It must mean something, he said, that you are all named for grandmothers or great-grandmothers.

"Well, what does it mean?" Ruby asked.

"He thinks we're ghosts," Evangeline said.

But Olive said, "It was just the way the schedule worked out. We were assigned to the same class in the same room at the same time. It was bound to happen."

"What a pedant you are," Evangeline said.

Evangeline's grandmother's name was, in fact, Bella, but she let the misapprehension stand. She had no wish to admit that she was stuck with Evangeline because it was her grandmother's favorite poem. Still, nothing could prevent George from declaiming the first twenty-two lines of it, which he had, in hoarse and secretive breaths, by heart. The rest of them could remember only the opening words: *This is the forest primeval.* Nowadays nobody quoted Longfellow, or even knew who he was. And they were all dumbstruck by George's acrobatic memory. This alone set him apart.

It lasted—the Pact—four years. Or it might have been four, had the Greek restaurant with the bluish fluorescent lights not in the interim been replaced by a used-car lot.

On that fourth year, only Evangeline showed up.

"It can't be a Pact if it's only the two of us," Evangeline said. "A Pact has to have several parties, like the Kellogg-Briand Pact, or the Triple Entente. It can't be just us."

They walked around the block, looking for a coffee shop. It was a shabby neighborhood, battered stucco houses with high stoops, noisy ragamuffins with their sticks and balls.

Ragamuffins was George's word. Evangeline noticed that he had taken on something like a British accent, though not quite. He looked different. Not that old student outfit, sweatshirt and jeans and no socks. He wore an actual suit, with a surprising vest that had a little pocket for an old-fashioned watch on a chain. The jacket was a showy tweed, with outmoded leather patches on the elbows and pimpled all over with forest-green nubbles. The patches were a bright orange worthy of parrots. His tie was diagonally striped, and it too had the look of obsolescence. He'd acquired the suit in New Zealand, he said, to look more like the New Zealanders. They were notorious swimmers, and in summer went about half naked, but otherwise they dressed like peacocks.

In the end, they found a dirty little park, more concrete than leafy, and sat on a bench sticky with bird droppings. But it could not be avoided: they spoke of the mundane and the pedestrian and the parochial—what had become of the defectors. Ruby had found a job as the librarian of an elementary school in an obscure Ohio town (population 1,396). Olive, who had settled in Chesapeake, Virginia, was already the mother of two little boys, and worked part-time in the local branch of the public library. She was no longer Olive; she had changed her name to Susan—talk of the mundane! And even Evangeline, who hadn't defected and remained loyal to the Pact, had to acknowledge that she was more chauffeur than librarian.

She drove a green truck outfitted with bookshelves to a far weedy corner of the Bronx, on the odorous edge of rusted railroad tracks.

But George had emigrated to New Zealand. His position there, he said, had a future. Though he was now on the middle rung of a great university library in Auckland, in five years, he predicted, he would be its director. It was an ingenuity of foresight that had landed him in the very first library to digitize, not only in New Zealand but in the world at large. New Zealand was a model, and it was in connection with this revolutionary transition that he had been sent as a liaison to New York on an errand that required discretion. His value was recognized. The director had arranged for him to stay at the Waldorf, certainly to facilitate meetings but also for his personal comfort.

Evangeline herself had an unexpected story to tell. In that forlorn neighborhood, where on Friday afternoons the clusters of children and their mothers were congregated under umbrellas (it seemed always to be raining), waiting for the green truck and its cargo, she too beheld her imminent good fortune. She had seen surveyors' chalkings on the pavements around a disused old comfort station marked for renovation. It was a low handsome concrete building in the style of a Greek temple; weathered carvings of Hygeia, the goddess of health, and Amphitrite, the goddess of waters, ran across the frieze below its pediment. From the look of it, you couldn't imagine that it had once housed public toilets. What it promised for Evangeline was that the truck with its dented fenders and its rain-damaged books would be cashiered, and she would soon be permitted to come indoors.

"An anointment," George said. "From bottom-feeder to kingfish." It meant, Evangeline knew, that he didn't think much of her prospects. She was letting down her solitary will.

They abandoned the bench and walked together to the train station. According to the Pact, its adherents were obliged to disperse immediately after the completion of the proceedings of the reunion; no one was to spy on the destination of the others. But it couldn't be helped: they had to board the same train, and because of the rush-hour crowding had to sit in the same car. George was heading for Grand Central in Manhattan to get to the Waldorf, and Evangeline for the Fordham stop in the Bronx. They had even found seats directly across the aisle.

Leaning over, Evangeline asked, "But we still haven't decided where to meet next time. Or when."

"Same date as always."

"How do you know you'll be able to come? Supposing the university doesn't send you?"

"As it happens, I have another reason. A family reason. I've told you about my uncle."

He had. He had told all three of them at their very first meeting in the Greek restaurant; he had told them every jot and tittle of what he called his blighted yet colorful bloodline. His parents were suicides. Side by side, like Stefan Zweig and his wife Lotte in Petrópolis, they had taken poison. He was then a child of two. He knew nothing about it for years, only that his mother and father weren't really his mother and father: they were his great-aunt and his great-uncle. They were both very old, and his aunt was dead. In their prime, they had been vaudevillians. Their closets were packed with stage apparel. George often had his dinners in the wings. The Waldorf was agreeable, he admitted, but he'd much prefer to stay with his unregenerate uncle, at ninety-nine still hankering after a gig.

None of the others knew where Petrópolis was. Olive guessed Greece, but Evangeline said, "Two suicides? One would be excessive, but two is exorbitant."

Ruby asked, "Is that Oscar Wilde?"

"Evangeline, how heartless you are," Olive said. Still, George didn't mind: the uncommon was his legacy. It was what he sought. He knew he was a sport, a daring mutation. He took his stand on the precipice of life, and if Evangeline wanted to mock, it was all right with him. He knew it was out of envy.

"Fine," Evangeline said, "same date, but where?"

"Same place."

"But there's nothing there!" she called as she stepped out of the car.

"There will be," he yelled back.

The newly constructed library had a laboratory look, sleek and metallic. It betrayed everything library school remembered. Gone were the wood-paneled walls, gone were the wooden drawers with their rows of handwritten index cards. Gone were the pencils with those overworked rubber date stamps on their tails. And gone were the footprints of winter boots (here they left no marks on the all-weather carpet), and, in summer, gone was the staccato creak of antique fans as they turned their necks from side to side. Instead: rows of computers with their cold faces, air-conditioners and their goosepimpling blasts. Polite young men with research degrees—Mouse One and Mouse Two—behind steel desks. Because of the double-glazed windows you could never smell the rain.

Evangeline blamed Hygeia and Amphitrite for permitting this invasion; they had since been removed as unfit for contemporary taste. The plumbing was new, the temple bare of its goddesses. Its visitors were called, condescendingly, customers, as if they were coming to argue over the cost of tomatoes in a market. The children's room was located in what had been the women's toilets, far from the hushed center. And unlike the shrieks and the tumult that had greeted the green truck when it veered into view, here it was disconcertingly quiet. Many of the customers seemed to be hobbyists, or half-insane cranks catching up on their sleep, or lonely browsers searching for spiritual succor.

The more typical customers came and went with their emptied plastic grocery bags newly loaded, but the hobbyists were the most persistent. They would arrive at ten in the morning and sit at the reading tables until four in the afternoon. They were mostly elderly widows copying needlepoint patterns, or genealogical enthusiasts hoping to find a royal ancestor, or backyard farmers who grew potatoes in pots and were looking into the possibility of beekeeping.

But one of these oddities appeared to be a generation younger than the rest, and turned up only one day a week, generally not long before closing. He was of middling height and habitually carried a worn canvas portfolio. He wore a seaman's cap—an affectation, Evangeline decided, meant to counteract mediocrity. He would spend no more than half an hour with a writing pad and—this was notable—a child's box of crayons, gazing at colorful photographs in sizable volumes and making notes. His subject was birds, she saw, each time a different bird. His drawings were moderately talented. He used every crayon in the box. Though he always arrived late in the day, he rarely overstayed; but once, hurrying to pack up when the lights were already switched off, he left behind one of his papers. It had slipped from the table to the floor, unnoticed.

Evangeline picked it up. It was a picture of a bird with pink legs and yellow breast feathers, and under it, in capital letters, SMALL-HEADED FLYCATCHER.

"I saved this for you," she told him the next time he came. "I thought you might be missing it."

"It's extinct," he said, "so it's really missing. You can only see it in Audubon."

"Are you an artist?" she asked, though she doubted it. He didn't have the look of an artist. He said he was interested in bird-watching, and it was only his amateur's illusion that he might someday spot an actual small-headed flycatcher. It turned out that he was a math teacher in a nearby high school. She asked him, politely, what subjects he taught. Elementary algebra, he said, intermediate algebra, geometry, trigonometry, spherical trigonometry, and, for the advanced students, introduction to calculus. His recitation was insistently precise.

After that she dismissed him as intolerably earnest. Even his drawings of each minute nostril hole in each beak testified to dogged monotony: beak after beak after beak, all with those tiny black specks. But he began arriving earlier, and lingered on, and now and then he approached her desk to display his latest work.

"This one," he explained, "is a blue mountain warbler, and look at this eastern pinnated grouse, it's really a species of prairie chicken. They're both extinct. Did you know what a butcher Audubon was? He killed thousands of birds to lay out their carcasses to paint."

And then he invited her to go bird-watching on the coming Sunday.

Looking up from her keyboard (Evangeline too was now digitized), she choked down a laugh. Was this middle-sized fellow in a seaman's cap courting her?

"I have an excellent pair of binoculars," he told her, "manufactured just outside of London. Very old firm, same outfit that makes the insides of grandfather clocks." He held out his hand in formal introduction. "Nate Vogel. Unfortunately, my name is a coincidence." And he added, in a voice she recognized as teacherly, "It means bird, you know."

Evangeline glanced down at her computer screen to check the date. September 26th. In three weeks it would be time for the Pact. She had already consulted her "Atlas of the Seven Continents" for Petrópolis (it was in Brazil), but what did she know of New Zealand? Nor would she come to George empty-handed, with nothing unusual of her own to tell.

On this ground she agreed to go bird-watching with Nate Vogel. After all, isn't the ludicrous also a kind of fanaticism, and must not the natural be made unnatural? And anyhow, she reflected, birds are the descendants of dinosaurs.

"You'd better put on your galoshes," he warned her.

"Where we're going the soil can be moist. It's only a short drive." But galoshes were what Evangeline's grandmother had worn when it snowed, and in the stifling dry heat of late summer sandals were good enough.

Their destination turned out to be a swamp. He led her through a watery forest of waist-high yellow-haired cattails where mosquitoes hovered in swarms, and showed her how to keep her head down so as to be camouflaged by the wild tangle of vegetation all around. The air was too dense to breathe, and the mud was seeping upward between her naked toes. Small thin snakes—or were they large fat worms—came crawling out of the nowhere of this dizzying shiver of living things.

Evangeline said, "My feet are drowning."

"Quiet, don't speak, it makes vibrations they can feel. See over there?" He passed her the binoculars. His whisper was as thin as a hiss. "It's a saltmarsh sparrow, nothing special, they're common around here."

"What am I supposed to look for?" she whispered back.

"You have to do your homework first. You have to be prepared."

"Prepared for what?"

"The thrill of identification."

What Evangeline saw was a bird. It was a bird like any other bird. And, like any other bird, it instantly flew away.

"Now look what you've done," he said. "I told you

not to speak. You've missed everything. Now we just have to wait."

Submissively, she handed back the binoculars. They sat side by side in silence, squatting in the wet. And then, disobeying his own rule, he explained exactly what she had missed: "The saltmarsh sparrow has a flat head with orange eyebrows and orange sidelocks and a speckled belly. The male is sexually promiscuous." Was this a direct quote from Audubon?

"I didn't know that birds are subject to moral standards," Evangeline said.

"Sh-h-h! There's another one. No, no, over there, to your left, quick, here, take the binoculars!"

This second bird was indistinguishable from the first. But now she knew what to look for: eyebrows and sidelocks, the thrill of identification. And she did feel a thrill, a horrible one. The bird was gazing at her with its single eye on the side of its flat head—a pterodactyl's cold indifferent Mesozoic eye.

They met again in the library on Monday afternoon. "I hope you enjoyed our little excursion yesterday," he said. "I hope you found it enlightening."

She decided to punish him. "I had to throw out my best sandals. They were soaked."

"What size are they? I'll be glad to get you a new pair."

But, instead, he brought her, on the following Monday, a small square box with a ribbon glued to its top.

Inside was a necklace with a pendant: a shiny miniature monocular.

"It isn't real silver," he informed her. "It's chrome, so it won't ever tarnish. I thought you'd like it as a memento."

He had come without his seaman's cap, and also without his crayons. Evangeline thought he looked somewhat taller in the absence of the cap, as if it had been squashing the top of his head. And it was true that his hair stood up like a hedge. It irritated her that his eyelashes were almost invisibly pale. He was one of those self-flattered men who were still as blond as young children. The memento she slipped into her purse, intending to forget it.

He said, "So how about dinner Thursday next week?"

"Sorry," Evangeline said. "I have a meeting in Stamford."

"What kind of meeting?"

"I do have a private life," she retorted.

"Fine, then the week after," he said.

Evangeline was pleased to have outwitted him—the Pact was set for Wednesday. But ornithology had anyhow enlightened her: George was a bird in the bush, and the bush was on the nether side of the globe. He had abandoned his natural habitat and had migrated to unknown skies and foreign seasons. Had he evolved to new instincts? In the space of a year she had almost forgotten the color of his eyes. She longed for the thrill of identification.

On the Internet she read:

New Zealand is an island country in the southwestern Pacific Ocean. The country geographically comprises two main landmasses and numerous smaller islands. Because of its remoteness, it was one of the last lands to be inhabited by humans. During its long period of isolation, New Zealand developed a biodiversity of animal, fungal, and plant life. Some time between 1250 and 1300 CE, Polynesian settlers arrived and adapted a distinctive Maori culture. In 1642, a Dutch explorer became the first European to sight New Zealand. Bats and some marine animals are the sole native mammals. Indigenous flora are abundant, including rimu, tawa, matai, rata, and tussock. High waters skirt forests, parks, and beaches.

But the Internet couldn't tell her whether George's eyes were brown or gray, or how and where he lived. Surely not in commonplace university housing. Then in a little shack (he would call it a cottage) on the rim of the fathomless Pacific, together with a Maori lover? She knew what "marine animals" meant. In the treacherous tides ringing the coast of New Zealand, the shadows of sharks, and also of dolphins. George would seek out the sharks.

The train to Stamford had empty seats; it was the middle of a weekday afternoon. And now the parking lot too was gone. Still, hadn't George, spurred by the ingenuity of foresight, promised that something, after all, would be there? And something was: a swarming and a roaring of dump trucks and cement mixers and steam shovels and muscular men in hard hats and hired ragamuffins handing out anti-gentrification leaflets, all surrounding a mammoth billboard with a picture of a very tall building and a newsworthy message in noisy purple and green paint:

```
COMING SOON
STAMFORD'S FINEST LUXURY
APARTMENTS
WATCH US RISE
```

But it was George she was watching for. Was he late, or was she too early? Or was it she who was late, and he'd given up and gone back to his suite at the Waldorf? Impossible; he wouldn't desert his most loyal adherent to the Pact. Or did he suppose that she, like the others, had succumbed to the hollow quotidian? A fine brown dust was beginning to thicken her throat. Her lips were coated with grit. Then it came to her how foolish she was: he knew better than to wait in a fog of dirt. He was expecting her to show up at their old bench.

The bench was missing most of its slats. The bird droppings had multiplied. And what species of bird might they be? There were owls in Connecticut; in one of his most careful drawings Nate Vogel had crayoned a long-eared one. It almost resembled a rabbit. The subtlety of its colorings had required three separate shades of gray: dun, dove, and dusk.

But George was not there. After an hour and a half, and by now it was two and a half, he still was not there. She pondered why. Doubtless the university had promoted him, and he was no longer, like some freshly recruited underling, sent abroad on a superfluous errand—wasn't it clear that the world was already sufficiently cyberized? Or might it be that the ancient great-uncle had died in his absence, and he had no further reason to turn his back on New Zealand? The Pact was the fruit of his own, his central—his necessary—passion. Why would he abandon it? It was the seed of his Idea.

On the train back to Fordham—it was again rush hour, and so crowded that she had to stand holding on to an overhead strap—she all at once saw his Idea. Or she felt it, like a thunder coursing through the churn of the blood in her skull. George had allowed himself to disappear, it was his solitary will at work, it was fanaticism's ultimate flourish. He meant to shock her, he meant to undo her expectation, he meant to disappoint and to betray. The shock of his disappearance was not a negation of the Pact; it was its electrifying fulfillment.

The next week she consented to have dinner with Nate Vogel. His original notion of Thursday was a mistake. He preferred Saturday night, the traditional time, he said, for a real date. Date? This was galoshes again: the last traces of her grandmother's era. He had discovered a nice little bar right here in the neighborhood, four or five blocks from the library. On a mild autumn evening, when the library closed early for the weekend, they could walk there. She dreaded his intention: the dark, the booze, the thumping beat of the piped-in rock, the side-by-side intimacy of bodies in close quarters.

On the way, he asked whether she knew that vegetarians lived longer than meat eaters. "Somewhere between six and ten percent," he said. "And here we are. This is the place. I tried it out before I broached it."

The sign on the window read HEALTH BAR. There were rows and rows of salads to choose from, and little round tables with artificial flowers at the center of each. The lights were bright. The music was Mozart. He said, "The avocado with persimmon is excellent."

But Evangeline ordered eggplant.

"Did you know," he said, "that the persimmon means change? Because it's bitter when it's green and sweet when it turns orange."

He gave her his most importuning look. His breath was close, too close, to her own. For the first time she observed his eyes; they were the color of one of his most frequently used crayons. It was labelled taupe. Evangeline wondered whether there might also be an esoteric crayon that matched George's eyes. Aubergine, perhaps, like earth's most beautifully sculptured fruit.

And now he put out a forefinger to touch her lips; was this a presumptuous prelude to a kiss?

It was not. How chaste he was!

"I can't help noticing," he said, "that you have the archaic smile. Do you know what that is? Let's go to the Met and I'll show you. Is next Sunday okay?"

He took her to the Greek and Roman galleries. On plinth after plinth, a procession of ancient stone heads, each with its meaningful yet inscrutable smile.

"It could be a sign of revelry," he said, "or it could be derision. Nobody really knows."

"I choose derision," Evangeline said.

"Let's go look at the Buddha smiles. To compare."

He led her through the Asian halls, and then to Egypt, evading the sarcophagi to search for pharaonic mirth.

"We think we've got the cream of the crop in the Mona Lisa," he said, "but look at Nefertiti! Did you know that her left eye is missing? It was made of quartz, but they've never found it."

They sat on the topmost steps in front of the Met.

The sun was abnormally hot for October, and the afternoon air had a dizzying haze. It seemed to Evangeline that they had walked endless miles, from one civilization to another. An ice cream cart was parked on the sidewalk below.

"Are you parched?" he asked, and came back with two orange popsicles. "Did you know how Indian summer got its name? From the Iroquois hunting season. Next time we could check out the local pinnipedia."

He was proposing an expedition to the Bronx Zoo. How wholesome he was!

They were leaning against the wrought-iron fence circling the sea lions' pool. The sea lions, sprawled on their boulders, too lethargic to dive, were all barking loudly in chorus. Against the din he said, "Do you know the difference between a seal and a sea lion? The sea lion has earflaps and can walk on its flippers. The seal has these apertures instead of ears and can only go on its belly. And did you know"—and here he grew excited—"that the hippopotamus evolved from the dolphin? In terms of aeons, it happened all of a sudden."

He bought her a balloon in the shape of a giraffe, and also two ice cream cones—her choice, one vanilla, one strawberry. But it was getting too cold for ice cream. Indian summer was over. They were both wearing sweaters. "And by the way," he said, "I hope you won't mind, but pretty soon I'll be moving out of the neighborhood."

"Why would you do that?" It came as a jolt to Evangeline that she was not indifferent to this announcement; somehow it embarrassed her. And why should she mind?

He had done his homework, he explained. Looked at all the want ads, asked around, got a tip about an opening in a well-funded private high school for girls, principal soon to retire, and so forth. All this was muddling: she had no inkling that Nate Vogel might be ambitious. How could a man so sure, so lacking in anxiety, so satisfied in his habits, so at home with equations, want to change his perfectly normal life? And no, he hadn't applied to the math department; he detested Euclid, he was sick of Pythagoras, he didn't care whether zero existed or not. Evangeline declined to believe him. For once he was making things up.

"It's in Connecticut," he told her. "The school. I got the job. It means a big jump in pay. And they like it that I do math. It's all about budgets."

How uninspired to be gratified by something so banal as running a fancy school! As if Connecticut were kin to the dolphin-thronged coast of New Zealand.

And then she remembered that implausibility is the true authenticity. Otherwise how could the hippopotamus have once been a dolphin?

And then she thought, He always means what he says. And everything he says is so.

And then she thought, How wholesome he is, how chaste!

And then she thought, Chaste needn't mean celibate.

Six months later, she married him. And like Hygeia and Amphitrite before her, she decamped. Mouse One and Mouse Two were anyhow at war, vying for head librarian. Mouse Two had turned tiger and, by virtue of clearing out the cranks who commandeered whole tables for their hobbies, had won. He would have ousted Nate Vogel.

The girls' school was located in the suburbs of Stamford. Evangeline could hardly admit to surprise; everything that happens is inevitable, evolution is sudden. They were given a perk, a little house of their own, set in an acre of greenery; it was called the Principal's House. Still, she regretted that swamps and zoos were behind them.

"Posh," Evangeline said. "And those silly uniforms the girls have to wear." She was thirty-seven years old, the age of the beginning of nostalgia, when early discontent becomes regret. She regretted the long-ago loss of the green truck. She regretted that Mouse Two now reigned in place of the goddesses of water and well-being. She regretted that George had so far receded in her longings that she not only couldn't recall the color of his eyes; his voice too with all its clairvoyance, had faded. The words survived, but not the clarion call. George was nearly beyond retrieval, a tiny glint of a mote, like a wayward flea.

She did not regret marrying Nate Vogel. They named the baby Bella, after Evangeline's grandmother. Together, they worked to suspend a shiny miniature mobile over Bella's little bed, where it wafted and twisted and fitfully caught the light. Bella gazed at it intelligently, though it was only a chrome monocular and not a real toy.

It was December. Evangeline liked to walk in the cold. Bella in her puffy swathings and Muscovite wool hat, under blankets in her carriage, was no more than an amorphous bundle. Evangeline wore furry Muscovite boots. A steamy cloud spilled out of her throat with every breath, but still she pushed the carriage everywhere, through unfamiliar streets and small icy plazas and rows of shops of every kind. She walked and walked: a private walk, a secret walk, secret even from Nate Vogel. And finally there it was, transfigured. Risen as pledged. It had renewed its surround, it had staunchly gentrified. Its fifteen luxury floors looked down on a lavish playground, where silky-cheeked children in thick winter regalia were bobbing on seesaws and shrieking down slides. Shivering nannies stood by. The ragamuffins were nowhere.

And next the bench. A different bench, stone sparkling with mica, impregnable to harm. Only the bird droppings were the same. Or were they? How do owls fare in December?

Bella was howling, and they were far from home, with miles to go. But Evangeline had seen what she wanted to see: that George was yet again not there.

April came, and Evangeline pushed Bella's stroller around the neighborhood, peering into the windows of stores. Trees grew all along the sidewalks. A bus snorted its way down the street. Bella pointed with her tiny finger and said "Buh." When a second bus followed in the fumy wake of the first, Bella pointed again and said "Buh-buh." She was already mastering arithmetic.

They passed a store with its door open; it was a bookshop going out of business, collateral damage of the new age of digital reading. Evangeline looked in. A man was on his knees, pulling books off their shelves and thrusting them into cardboard boxes. She could see only his elbows as he bent forward to the lowest shelf. He was wearing a nubbly tweed jacket; the elbow patches were of leather worn into creases, the color of ripened persimmon. When he stood and showed his face, it was again not George.

Nate Vogel was content. Every morning at breakfast the chatter of flocks of adolescent girls came to them through the open windows like undulating notes of nightingales. "What a pity," he said, "there aren't any nightingales around here. Not a single one. They winter in Africa and summer in Europe." He had looked up the history of the Principal's House. The school was founded just before the Battle of Appomattox. "Did you know," he said (and she was sometimes attentive), "that it was used by the Underground Railroad?" He no longer wore his seaman's cap; it was unsuitable for his office, it had no dignity. His hair stood up, an unplowed harvest, an improbable wheat field.

Bella too was content. Now she was mastering the art of two-leggedness.

One night in a dream Evangeline understood why she couldn't remember the color of George's eyes. They were colorless. A white light streamed out of them, turning everything translucent. When she awoke, she was uncertain of the meaning of her conscious life: was she no different from Ruby and Susan (formerly Olive), or was she, in truth, burning always with the hard, gemlike flame of her solitary will?